Torchlight

Torchlight

Carol Otis Hurst

Houghton Mifflin Company Boston 2006

Walter Lorraine Books

Walter Lorraine [logo] Books

www.houghtonmifflinbooks.com

Library of Congress Cataloging-in-Publication Data

Hurst, Carol Otis.
  Torchlight / Carol Otis Hurst.
    p. cm.
  Summary: In 1864, fifth-grader Charlotte befriends an Irish-American
girl at school and tries to understand the prejudices between the Irish
and the Yankees in her town of Westfield, Massachusetts. Based on
historical events.
  ISBN-13: 978-0-618-27601-1
  ISBN-10: 0-618-27601-7
  1. Irish Americans—Juvenile fiction. [1. Irish Americans—Fiction.
2. Prejudices—Fiction. 3. Friendship—Fiction. 4. Schools—Fiction.
5. Massachusetts—History—19th century—Fiction.] I. Title.
PZ7.H95678Tor 2006
[Fic]—dc22
                                                          2005036556

Printed in the United States of America
MP 10 9 8 7 6 5 4 3 2 1

For Cooper Marsh

CONTENTS

Author's Note

This story is based on a real incident:

In July, 1854, the partly complete [Catholic] church was threatened by a mob advancing to burn it. They were dissuaded by an eloquent speech by Hiram Hull, a Protestant with considerable influence.

Ella Wallace
Westfield Massachusetts 1669–1969
Westfield Tri-Centennial Association, Inc.
1968

At the time of this story, Westfield, a small town in the foothills of the Berkshire Mountains of

Massachusetts, had two—and only two—groups of citizens: Yankees and Irish.

The Yankees were from England and Scotland, and many of them had been in America for a very long time. Irish men had come to the area to help build the Northampton New Haven Canal. That canal was supposed to bring lots of business to the area, but it failed, mostly because the railroads were coming, and trains were easier and cheaper to run. Lots of people lost money on the canal, including many of the Irish laborers who had agreed to take their wages in shares of the canal. When it came time to lay the track for the railroads, Irish laborers were needed again.

Many of the Irish men sent for their families and settled in towns up and down the canal. When the potato famine began in Ireland, more Irish families came to western Massachusetts.

The strange thing is that, although people from many different countries settled in towns all around Westfield, according to the U.S. Census of 1850, 7,000 people were living in Westfield: 5,000 Yankees and 2,000 Irish, and nobody else.

The Yankees were, for the most part, Congregationalist Protestants. Most of the Irish were

Catholic. The Yankees owned more of the land, the money, and the power. The Irish took whatever work they could find.

Then, in 1854, the Irish wanted to build their own church. One of the Yankees, Samuel Fowler, gave them some land to build it on, but many Yankees didn't want a Catholic church in "their" town.

And there was another reason for people to be upset. Until that time, most of the children in Westfield went to one-room schools that were scattered around the various neighborhoods. So Irish kids and Yankee kids went to separate schools where children from the first to eighth grades were in the same room. In 1854 the town decided it would be better to have fewer but bigger schools. That way there could be separate classrooms for younger and older students. This meant that, for the first time, Irish and Yankee children would be going to elementary school in the same building.

Most children, both Yankees and Irish, went no further than eighth grade. For the few whose parents could afford it and thought that a high school education was necessary, Westfield had a private school, the Westfield Academy.

This was the age of the horse-drawn carriage, and buggy whips were essential. Westfield was known as Whip City because of all the whips produced there. By 1865, there were thirty whip factories in town.

Hiram Hull, mentioned in the above quotation, was the owner of the largest whip factory in town, having invented a process by which raffia could be used in whip making. Hiram's wife's name was Lucy. As far as I could find out, Hiram and Lucy Hull had no children.

Now you have the facts. Everything else in the pages you are about to read is from my imagination. I made up all the people except for Hiram and Lucy Hull and Samuel Fowler, although I did use a lot of the last names of people living in Westfield at the time of the story. I've changed the timing of the story from July to the fall of 1854 so that I could include the school consolidation as a more obvious part of the problem.

Torchlight

1

Maggie

You can't be Irish!"

"I can't?"

"Your name's wrong."

"It is?"

"Irish people have an 'O' or a 'Mc' at the beginning of their names."

"Like Murphy, Sullivan, and Delaney, you mean?"

"Are those Irish names?"

"They are."

"You don't talk like the Irish do."

"How do they talk?"

"I don't know. Funny like."

"I was born here, Charlotte. I can even say 'Eh-ya' like you Yankees do."

"We say 'Eh-yah?'"

"Eh-yah. Why do you say that? It isn't even in the dictionary. How do you spell it?"

"I don't know. I guess we do say 'Eh-yah' sometimes. Don't you?"

"Only when I'm making fun of Yankees."

"Did you know I was a Yankee, Maggie?"

"I did."

"How?"

"By that mark on your forehead."

"I don't have a mark on my forehead."

"That was a joke, Charlotte."

"Be serious. How did you know?"

"Because I know all the Irish—at least by sight—and in Westfield, if you're not Irish, you're Yankee."

"I guess that's true."

"If you had known I was Irish, would you have played with me that first day?"

Maggie

"I don't know. I didn't think there would be Irish children here."

"It's 1854, Charlotte—not the Dark Ages. No more one-room schools in Westfield. Bigger schools, bigger districts, and here we are together like beans in a pot."

"That's the bell."

"Best we get in line then."

"Eh-yah."

&

That afternoon, on her way home from school, Charlotte smiled to herself, remembering that first real conversation with Maggie.

Heading to the new school on the first day of school three days earlier, Charlotte had a far different expression on her face. She had been lonely and a little bit scared.

Zach wouldn't have walked to school with her anyway, but other years he'd have been in the crowd somewhere. That would have been a comfort, but Zach had left early for the Academy, eager to begin high school. As she drew nearer the new Green District School, Charlotte could see more and more children, but she was the only one walking alone.

She wondered if people watching from their windows were feeling sorry for her. "There's that Charlotte Hodge all by herself again. She must not have any friends. Poor thing." Charlotte had put on a broad smile. That way people would think she chose to walk alone. But what if they thought she looked foolish walking along with an idiot smile on her face? She had stopped smiling and put on an expression that she hoped looked intelligent—much too intelligent to want or need company.

Carrie Beech and Susan Baker might have walked to school with her, but Carrie had moved to Springfield last summer; Susan's family had gone west. Her father had left for California a year ago, and he'd sent for the whole family to come join him. Charlotte guessed she couldn't really call Susan or Carrie friends anyway. She'd had friends in Agawam though, hadn't she? Minnie, one of them was, and Chella was another. What were their last names? Was it Minnie Brown, maybe? Charlotte was having trouble remembering lots of things about her life in Agawam. Even the faces of her mother and father were getting harder to recall. She had worked at it a bit as she walked on that first day, sketching in her mind the color of their hair, the way her father's moustache was shaped. Her father was easier because of that moustache, but she had trouble filling in the face behind it. Her mother, though. What color were her mother's eyes?

As she reached the school, Charlotte saw that Ann Turner and her group had already gathered over by the fence. Charlotte had given up trying to be friends with them a long time ago. Their parents were friends of Aunt Lucy and Uncle Hiram, so Charlotte had tried—really tried—to make them like her when she first came to Westfield. She didn't know why they hated her, but they had made it very clear from the beginning that they did.

In the schoolyard, more children had gathered in groups, chattering excitedly. Charlotte walked slowly toward a spot close to a door that had a sign etched into the cement over it: GIRLS. She leaned against the side of the building and watched the pigeons swoop down to peck for food on the flattened grass. Some gathered in groups, but one walked alone. She wondered if it had done something unpigeonly and wasn't allowed to peck with the others. She wondered if it knew what it was it had done.

The bell rang, and Charlotte joined the other students forming lines at the doors—girls at one entrance, boys at the other. There were stairs leading to a large door in the middle. That one must be for teachers and other grownups. Everybody looked nervous, and most were staring straight ahead. Then a girl turned to smile right at Charlotte. At first Charlotte thought the girl must be smiling at someone behind her, and the girl's smile grew as Charlotte twisted around to check. It was a nice smile—not the least bit silly. Charlotte smiled back, and the girl moved her fingers in a tiny wave.

Everything inside the new school building was clean and shiny. The classroom was large, with rows of desks and attached chairs bolted to the floor. It seemed strange to see all those desktops and not an initial carved in a single one. What was there about a wooden surface that made boys pull out their jackknives and begin to carve no matter what the penalty? Charlotte's desk in the old school was so scarred that she had had to put a book underneath her papers to keep bumps out of her writing.

Charlotte and that smiling girl were given seats in a fifth-grade row with only Zenas Clark between them. Fourth graders were in the front, fifth graders in the middle, and sixth graders at the back. The first, second, and third graders were in a room across the hall, and the seventh and eighth graders were upstairs.

Charlotte thought she'd miss hearing the little ones as they learned to read and do their sums, but she felt very grown-up in this room full of upper graders.

She leaned forward to exchange smiles with the new girl, who put her finger in the hole in the upper right corner of her desk and raised her eyebrows at Charlotte. Charlotte pointed toward a large bottle of ink and the box of tiny glass wells on the teacher's desk. The girl nodded and smiled again.

Any minute, Charlotte knew, the teacher would hand out the writing supplies and carefully fill each tiny inkwell. Charlotte imagined herself inserting the new pen point into the holder, dipping it just far enough into the well so that the ink barely touched the tiny hole on the nib, and then writing her name: Charlotte Hodge. She'd been practicing her signature the last few evenings at her uncle's desk at home, trying to make the letters loop and flow into each other the way his writing did.

"Charlotte Hodge?"

Yes, Charlotte Hodge is what she'd write. Maybe even Charlotte Alice Hodge. She'd try to do it without a single blot, making the pen glide across the page, and the teacher would say . . .

"Charlotte Hodge?" Charlotte nodded. Yes, the teacher would read out her name and show everyone how beautifully she had written it.

"Charlotte Hodge!"

Good heavens! Miss Avery was frowning at her. What had she done? How could she be in trouble already?

"Charlotte Hodge, are you present?" Miss Avery held a red roll book and pencil.

Charlotte stood up, trying to ignore the giggles. Her face was probably beet red. "Present," she said. For a moment Charlotte just stood there, staring at the teacher.

"Thank you, Charlotte. You may sit down now."

She seemed to have forgotten how to sit. As the laughter grew, she sank into her seat.

Charlotte kept her head down as the routine of names called and answered continued.

"Annis Huntington?"

"Present."

"Avery Lane?"

"Present."

"Eunice Leffingwell?"

"Present."

"James Murphy?"

"Present."

"Margaret Nolan?"

Charlotte looked up as the girl who had waved at her stood. "Present," she said, sitting quickly down again. Margaret. Her name was Margaret.

At recess Margaret held up a small rubber ball and cocked her head toward the brick side of the building. And so they played Russia, taking turns throwing the ball against bricks in the required sequence: one clap before catching, two claps and a hand roll, three claps and a turnaround.

Charlotte didn't know why that particular game was called Russia. There was nothing Russian about it that she could see. Maybe it came from

Russia. There was another one called Swedish. She pictured the games starting in those faraway countries and being passed from child to child. But how would the games cross the ocean to Massachusetts? Perhaps sailors brought them. She imagined sailors on board a ship throwing the ball and clapping their hands under their legs as they did so. She giggled at the image.

"Charlotte? Quit your dreaming. It's your turn." Margaret was holding out the ball and laughing at her. Charlotte grinned and took the ball.

"You sound like my brother," Charlotte said.

"That's what he's always telling me."

"That it's your turn?"

"No, silly, that I should quit my dreaming and pay attention to what's going on."

After that, it had just seemed natural to head to the same spot together when they came back from the dinner hour. For three days Charlotte didn't know or care what the other girls were doing. She had a friend named Margaret.

"Playing with the Yank again, Maggie?" Kathleen McGuire asked as they headed to the brick wall on the fourth morning.

"Right as rain you are," Margaret said and

threw the ball for ones. "Want to join us?"

"That'll be the day," Kathleen called out as she ran toward a group of girls over by the fence.

"I thought your name was Margaret," Charlotte said.

"It is."

"Then why did she call you Maggie?"

"Most folks do. Except for teachers."

"Shall I call you Maggie then?"

"Call me anything but late for supper."

Charlotte smiled. Margaret—Maggie. Maggie sounded friendlier. She would call her new friend Maggie. Charlotte had often wished that she had a nickname. Zachary had Zach, but there was no nickname for Charlotte. Char? Charrie? No. Sometimes Uncle Hiram called her Peanut. Charlotte didn't mind that. In fact, she liked it, but it wasn't a name she wanted others to use. Charlotte watched Maggie go through to sevens and miss on the under-leg clap at eight.

What would Aunt Lucy think of her new friend? She was always telling Charlotte to bring someone home from school. What would happen if she brought Maggie? Would Aunt Lucy know right away that Maggie was Irish? Charlotte looked

Maggie over carefully. Her hair was about the same shade of brown as Charlotte's own, although Maggie's hair was curly and Charlotte's certainly was not. Maggie's eyes were blue, Charlotte's were brown; but Ann Turner had blue eyes, and she wasn't Irish. How could a person know?

"Of course they're your friends," Aunt Lucy had said when Charlotte tried to explain why she couldn't bring home anyone from Ann's group.

"Why, the Turners and Deweys call on us often, and we always return the visits. Mrs. Turner and Mrs. Dewey were both here last week putting up the last of the blueberries. And at the quilting bee, remember? You girls all helped. And Mr. Turner and your uncle play chess together most Friday nights. Those girls have been here with their parents many times."

Yes, they certainly had. Charlotte remembered those occasions well. Everybody chattered away during the meal or the work as if they were the best of friends, but once the children were excused, Zach would go out to be with his own friends, and the girls were off by themselves, all pretense of friendship vanished. They made fun of her. They said mean things. Usually Ann would start it. One night they nearly destroyed her scrapbook of pressed leaves.

Now Charlotte tried to imagine Maggie at their supper table. Would Maggie tell them she was Irish? Probably. She didn't seem the least bit ashamed of it. Would Aunt Lucy even talk to her? Would Uncle Hiram?

These days the supper-table conversation was often about the Irish, and Charlotte listened more attentively, now that she knew a real Irish person.

"A lady can't even walk at night on Rum Row anymore thanks to those drunken Irish at the saloons," Aunt Lucy had said last evening.

Lately many people had taken to calling a section of Court Street Rum Row because of the saloons that had sprung up near Park Square.

Uncle Hiram, carving the roast, raised his eyebrows. "Why, Lucy, I hadn't realized you wanted to walk on Rum Row. You should have told me, my dear," he said. "I'll walk with you there anytime. We could spend a lovely evening in one of the saloons—maybe even sing a bit. They've a good piano player at Fuller's. I'm sure those at the bar would appreciate your lovely alto voice. Do you know the words to 'Molly Malone'?"

"Hiram!"

But there was no stopping Uncle Hiram. "Of course, you'd have to use the ladies' entrance and not sit at the bar. Would that bother you, Lucy?"

Charlotte giggled, and Zachary laughed out loud, earning their aunt's warning glance, but the thought of Aunt Lucy sitting at a bar was just too funny. Mrs. Hull was a teetotaler and an active member of the Women's Temperance Union. She'd never go anywhere near a bar.

Uncle Hiram, on the other hand, often had a glass of whiskey at his desk when he went over business papers in the evening. Although her aunt never objected directly, she made her feelings on the evils of liquor quite clear.

After listening to one of Aunt Lucy's tirades on the subject, Charlotte had watched her uncle carefully for several nights, trying to see what evil effect his drink had, but he seemed the same after as before his whiskey. Charlotte couldn't recall seeing either her mother or her father take a drink. Perhaps they had been teetotalers too.

"Well, they ought to put a stop to it," Mrs. Hull declared.

"To the saloon or to the Irish going there?" Uncle Hiram continued to place the thick slices of beef on the platter as he teased his wife.

"This is not a laughing matter, Hiram." She gave another stern glance at the children. "The Irish are everywhere now—in the streets, in the shops. They should keep to their own."

"Their own streets and shops? Do they have any?"

"I don't know about shops," Aunt Lucy said, "but they've taken over Meadow Street and most of Prospect Hill. You'd think one of them would have ambition enough to start up a shop over there."

"Takes money to open a business, Lucy," her husband said, "even a very small one."

"There are lots of Irish children in the new school," Charlotte offered tentatively.

"And don't think I didn't try to stop that," Mrs. Hull said, "but, as usual, I got nowhere. Putting Irish children in a Yankee school is asking for trouble. If you had spoken up, Hiram, the board would have listened to you. But would you go with me to the meetings?" She shook her head. "Not for love nor money."

Mr. Hull smiled broadly. "I don't recall either one being offered, my dear. *Hmm.* Love or money. Which would I have chosen? Who knows where that could have led?"

"Hiram! The children!" Mrs. Hull glanced from one to the other, her face red with embarrassment.

Charlotte loved it when Uncle Hiram teased Aunt Lucy. When Charlotte and Zachary first came to live here, she had had difficulty understanding that Uncle Hiram and even Aunt Lucy sometimes said things just to be funny. Often they did it with smiles on their faces so it was easy to tell, but other times they kidded with straight faces. Maggie did that sometimes too—like when she said that Yankees had marks on their foreheads. Charlotte tried joking occasionally, but it never really worked. People just looked puzzled, and they didn't laugh or smile, even when she explained that she had been joking.

"There are six Irish boys and one Irish girl in the Academy," Zachary said.

"In the Academy? What's an Irish girl going to do with a high school education?" Aunt Lucy shook her head. "How can that be, Hiram? It costs money to go to the Academy, and there are standards. Surely those Irish children lack the background. They'll never be able to keep up. And none of the Irish have much money, do they?"

Uncle Hiram shook his head. "These are hard times. Some things in Westfield are opening up, but it's still not easy for people to find work. And it's even harder for the Irish to get a job—all those 'No Irish Need Apply' signs on shop windows, even on the fences of some farms." He passed the platter to his nephew. "I hire as many as I can, but things are slow to pick up."

Hiram Hull's whip factory was on the other side of town by the river. Westfield had several whip factories, but Uncle Hiram's was the largest. Charlotte often wondered why there were so many whip factories in Westfield. Was there something about the town that made whip makers come, or had one person set up a whip factory and all the others copied it because they couldn't think of anything else to make? She'd have thought someone could have come up with something else. If she owned a factory, she'd make something much more interesting than whips. *Hats*, she thought, *all kinds of hats.* She pictured herself sitting in an office like Uncle Hiram's, but with hats and ribbons and plumes all over the desk.

"But they can't earn much on the line, Hiram. Surely you have no Irish managers in the factory." Aunt Lucy paused with the serving spoon raised.

"Not yet," her husband agreed. "But soon, I think."

"You can't be serious. There'll be trouble if you do, Hiram."

Hiram Hull shrugged. "That's why I haven't done it yet, but Mike Nolan's a good man. He deserves the promotion. And Pat Philips and Sean O'Brien aren't far behind. I had to fire John Marshall. He came in drunk again."

"It's the Irish."

"The Irish got John Marshall drunk?" Mr. Hull chuckled.

"Like as not."

"John Marshall needs no help getting drunk. He does well enough on his own."

"Irish in the Academy," Mrs. Hull retreated to firmer ground as she adjusted her lace collar. "Why, the only place without them these days, thank the Heavenly Father, is the church."

"Yes, my dear, I think you can be sure that the Congregational church is safe from any Irish assault." Uncle Hiram sat down, tucked his napkin under his chin, and picked up his fork and knife.

Charlotte smiled at the thought of the Irish assaulting their church.

"The grace," Aunt Lucy reminded them all.

Her uncle nodded and bowed his head. "Bless this food to our use and us to thy service. Amen."

"Amen," Zachary and Aunt Lucy murmured, but Charlotte was lost in a mental image: she was sitting in the Hull pew listening to the Reverend Cooper going on and on about the wages of sin, and suddenly the big oaken doors of the church were flung open as crowds of Irish dashed inside, brandishing what? Beer mugs, perhaps. Reverend Cooper would stop in midsentence. Maybe all the Irish would be wearing her factory-made hats. The thought made her smile broader.

"Whit Warren says they're going to build their own church," Zachary observed as he spooned some corn onto his plate and passed the dish to his uncle. Merging that information with the image in her head, Charlotte pictured the Irish setting their beer mugs on the pews and grabbing up hammers and saws.

"Their own church? A papist church in Westfield? I think not." Aunt Lucy took up the gravy boat and poured some on her beef before passing it to Zachary. "We let them use the town hall for their service. Why would they need a church?"

"That was years ago, Lucy, and they did that for only a few weeks," her husband said. "It just didn't work out. They want their own place."

"They have their own place—in Ireland."

"Lucy." Uncle Hiram's glance at his wife was disappointed.

"Well, really, Hiram, you must do something. They're trying to take over Westfield."

Charlotte's image continued, now including her aunt's statement. The Irish had left the Congregational church and were marching on the town hall, saws in one hand and hammers in the other, her hats bobbing on their heads.

"All I know is what Whit said." Zachary helped himself to gravy. "He said they want to build on that lot on Bartlett Street."

Aunt Lucy frowned. "Which lot?"

"The one on the corner of Meadow."

"Well, there's no chance of that." Her frown disappeared. "We own that lot. That's one spot safe from the Irish."

Charlotte pictured the hammer-and-saw-bearing, hat-wearing Irish clustered around a sign on the vacant lot: No Irish Need Apply.

"Charlotte!" her brother spoke sharply, and the empty lot, the sign, the hats, and the Irish vanished. "Quit sitting there dreaming with that silly grin on your face. Take the gravy and pass it on."

❧

Charlotte knocked on Zachary's door that night on her way to bed. Aunt Lucy and Uncle Hiram were reading downstairs.

"Come in, Charlotte," Zachary said.

"How did you know it was me?" she asked, stepping into the room.

Zach grinned at her from his seat at the table he used for a desk. "Easy guess," he said.

"How is school?" she asked.

"It's all right," he replied.

"Is it hard?"

"Not yet, but it's going to be," he said. "I've got

algebra, astronomy, rhetoric. And, as if that's not enough, there's Latin and Greek. Already I get them mixed up and we've barely started."

"What's it like?"

"Latin and Greek?"

"No. The Academy."

"Busy. Noisy between classes with everybody rushing to the next one. I got lost twice."

"Zach," she said. "Do you remember what Mother and Father looked like?"

"Of course," he said quickly. Then, after a pause, "Don't you?"

"Sure," she said. "Sure, I do. Good night, Zach."

2

Taking Over Westfield

Do you really want to take over Westfield, Maggie?"

"Me? What would I do with it if I took it, Charlotte?"

"No, not YOU you. I mean you Irish you."

"How would we Irish we do that?"

"I don't know. My aunt says you Irish are trying to take over Westfield."

"Your aunt talks a lot to the Irish, does she?"

"No, but—"

"Does your aunt even know any Irish? To speak to, I mean."

"Of course she does."

"Who?"

"She talks to our housemaid, Bridget. She's Irish."

"You have a maid?"

"Eh-yah. But she comes in only a few hours a day. She's not a live-in."

"Poor you. And Bridget wants to take over Westfield? Does she have plans for it?"

"Be serious, Maggie. Zachary says you're going to build an Irish church."

"You'd rather we come to yours?"

"Probably not. It's pretty full of Yankees."

"Do all Yankees go to that church?"

"Everybody I know does."

"Don't all you Yankees know each other?"

"Well, no. I don't think so. Maybe my aunt and uncle do. There are a lot of us."

"There certainly are."

"Are all Irish Catholic?"

"Everyone I know is."

"And you know all the Irish in Westfield."

"Pretty much."

"*You wouldn't like our church anyway, Maggie. We don't pray to the Pope. We pray to God.*"

"*So do we, Charlotte.*"

"*You'll do anything the Pope says to do. That's a fact, isn't it?*"

"*And the Pope wants us to take over Westfield? He has plans for it, does he?*"

"*Oh, I don't know. You missed. My turn.*"

❧

Charlotte stopped at Huntington's Yard Goods on the way home from school that afternoon. She liked being sent for sewing supplies. Looking at the shelves full of beautiful patterns and colors was always fun.

She fingered a piece of rose satin on her way to the lace shelf. Wouldn't that black lace with the flowers look lovely against the rose satin? It was nothing she would wear, of course, not now, but when she was grownup, that would make a perfect ball gown.

She pictured herself in rose satin and black lace. Big hoops were fashionable now. She'd have big hoops under this gown so that the skirt stuck way, way out. How did women sit with those big hoops? Well, she wouldn't be sitting anyway. She'd be dancing. There'd be a dance program all filled out, of course, dangling from her wrist as she glided across the floor with a handsome young man. What would his name be? Henry, perhaps. Or Thomas. Yes, that's it. His name would be Thomas. Thomas would compliment her on how well she danced.

She'd have to learn to dance. Who would teach her? Did Uncle Hiram and Aunt Lucy know how? She tried to picture them gliding around a ballroom. But Aunt Lucy was embarrassed when Uncle Hiram even kissed her on the cheek. "Hiram, the children," she'd say as she pushed him away. How could they possibly dance? Even in the quadrille people had to touch each other. Charlotte sighed and went on down the aisle.

Here was what her aunt wanted—white lace in a peony pattern. Half a yard, she had said. Charlotte brought the roll over to the counter where two women stood in line. One had her arms full of bolts of cloth. The other had a card of buttons. The two women stepped back as Charlotte approached. *They must be Irish.*

Mrs. Huntington smiled at Charlotte and took the lace from her hand.

"That's a lovely pattern. How much did you want?" she asked.

A bolt of cloth slid from the arm of the woman nearest Charlotte. Charlotte caught it before it hit the floor and handed it back.

The woman smiled as she readjusted her load. "Thank you, dearie," she said.

Mrs. Huntington continued to look straight at Charlotte. "How much do you want?"

"Just half a yard, please."

Mrs. Huntington measured the length of lace from her nose to her outstretched left hand. She picked up the scissors and cut half the measured amount of the lace. "Ten cents," she said, wrapping the lace carefully in brown paper.

Charlotte handed her the dime, took the lace, and left the store. She headed down Broad Street, her schoolbooks tucked under one arm, the lace in her other hand.

She loved the trees that lined this street. They were not the common maples and elms that were in the tree belt on most other streets in Westfield but catalpa, gingko, and lacy maple. *How did such trees come to be here?* She pictured an early settler, having traveled the world looking for just the right trees, arriving in Westfield and unloading his covered wagon full of saplings. Why had he chosen Broad Street for the planting? Perhaps it was because the houses on Broad Street were as wonderful as the trees that guarded them, but maybe the trees had come first, and people tried to build homes as beautiful as the trees.

The Lane house had a red roof, and the first floor was done not in brick but in a kind of cement with traprock stuck into it. The Lanes owned the traprock quarry on East Mountain, so Charlotte thought of their house as a kind of advertisement for their business. "See what you can do with traprock," it seemed to say. "Buy some now."

The Avery house was white clapboard with dark red trim. Two large windows on the second floor looked like eyes, with the porch a big smile underneath them. When the top shutters in those windows were closed, the house seemed to smile sleepily. When both sets of shutters were open, it was wide awake. She'd never seen both the top and bottom shutters closed. That, she supposed, would make the house seem to be smiling in its sleep. If she owned that house, she'd put in a smaller window above the porch to add a nose to the face. She'd also want a bell hanging on the porch to be used to wake up the house if it slept too long.

The Kittredge house was square. It had a side yard with a small fountain in the center. Mrs. Kittredge was a good gardener, and it was always a pleasure to look at the flowers. This time of year, the whole yard bloomed with chrysanthemums and marigolds in shades of white, gold, and russet, and salvia added its vivid red borders. Charlotte paused a moment just to enjoy the sight.

All the houses on Broad Street were quite lovely, but none was as wonderful as the Hulls'. That house stood at the very end of the street, facing Broad but really on Silver Street. It was three stories high, with a walk that curved up to the front door and then back to the street, making the shape of a horseshoe. In the center of the lawn stood a small girl and boy, their arms around each other. The stone children looked down at a tiny pool where the birds came to drink and to bathe.

Charlotte had named those children Thomas and Rachel. She wondered if they liked their constant view of the pool, or if they sometimes longed to look up at the sky. She always greeted them when she came up the walk, and sometimes, if she thought they seemed lonely, she stopped to tell them about her day.

There were seven kinds of trees on the land surrounding the house: blue spruce, white pine, Chinese maple, beech, chestnut, horse chestnut, and crab apple. Charlotte spent a lot of time during the summer in her favorite crab apple tree reading or thinking or just watching the birds. The leaves kept her perch hidden from passersby.

She tried to remember the house in Agawam. It had been small, with houses close on either side. How many rooms did it have? *Four,* she thought, *if you counted the summer kitchen.* There'd been a large birch tree in the backyard. Come to think of it, maybe it had been a beech tree.

She wondered what kind of houses those women in the store lived in. Someday she would take a walk down Meadow Street and look at Irish houses. Bridget lived on Meadow Street. Maybe those women in the store were Bridget's neighbors. Or Maggie's. At any rate, Maggie must know them. She said she knew all the Irish in Westfield.

Charlotte must remember to ask Maggie what street she lived on.

Her thoughts turned back to the women in the store. How long had that woman with her arms full of cloth been waiting? "Yankees first" had never bothered Charlotte before, but that much cloth was surely a bigger purchase than her own tiny bit of lace and much more expensive. The Irish woman should at least have been able to put the bolts down on the counter. Maybe there was a law. Maybe shopkeepers had to wait on Yankees first no matter what the size of the sale was.

She pictured a courtroom where a judge sat looking down at a weeping Mrs. Huntington. "Fifty days for serving an Irish woman first!" he said as he brought down his gavel.

Charlotte shivered. The weather had turned chilly. Already the chestnut was showing some color, and the gingko showed tiny bits of the brilliant yellow to come. In a few weeks they'd all be wearing fall colors. She was too cold for a long chat with Rachel and Thomas this afternoon, but she couldn't resist a few words.

"I have a friend," she told them, leaning down to look into their faces. She thought they seemed pleased. She gave a quick glance around. "She's Irish," she whispered and ran up the steps.

"I'm home!" she shouted as she opened the door.

❧

At breakfast Charlotte asked, "Is it a law about the Irish?"

"About what, dear?" Aunt Lucy passed her the sausage platter.

"Is it a law that they can't be waited on first?"

"No, it's not a law," Uncle Hiram said. "It's just custom. We were here first. We get waited on first."

"So, do Indians get waited on before Yankees?" Uncle Hiram laughed. "You'd have to go out west to find that out, Peanut. There are no Indians left around here."

"But when the Yankees first came here, did they have to wait for the Indians to be waited on?" Charlotte asked.

"Of course not," Zach answered. "No one waited on the Indians."

"But shouldn't Irish women get waited on before Bridget came in with the coffee.

Yankee children?" Charlotte asked. "Aren't we supposed to respect our elders?"

No one answered.

After Bridget left the room, Aunt Lucy said, "Don't talk about the Irish in front of Bridget, dear. It might hurt her feelings."

3

Meadow Street

"Are your aunt and uncle nice?"

"Oh, yes. Very."

"How long have you lived with them?"

"Since I was seven."

"Do your mother and father live there too?"

"No—they died."

"What of?"

"Cholera."

"Both at once?"

"Almost."

"I'm sorry, Charlotte. It must be terrible to lose your parents."

"Eh-yah."

"Did you move in with your aunt and uncle as soon as your parents were gone?"

"They brought us here right after the funeral."

"Weren't they afraid of catching the cholera?"

"I don't know. Aunt Lucy came as soon as she heard they were sick and stayed until . . . until after."

"What's it like living in that big house?"

"You know where I live, Maggie?"

"Everybody knows where the Hulls live."

"It's nice. There's a big silver beech tree right outside my window.'"

"Never mind the trees. Tell me about the house. Do you have your own room?"

"You don't?"

"I'm lucky to have my own bed."

"What color is your house?"

"Gray."

"Where is it?"

"On Meadow Street."

"What's it like?"

"Meadow Street?"

"No, silly, your house."

"Crowded. Noisy. Everybody seems to want to be in the same place at once."

"How many brothers and sisters do you have?"

"There are six of us—four boys at the top and then Maureen and me."

"Where's Maureen?"

"In the primary room. How many do you have?"

"Just Zach and me."

"That must be peaceful."

"I guess. But it must be fun having all those people to talk to. I'll bet you never get lonely."

"Lonely? Mam says the privy's the only place to think your own thoughts, and then only if you hurry."

"Who's Mam?"

"My mother."

"Why do you call her Mam?"

"I don't know. We all do. Mam and Da."

"I don't think those words are in the dictionary, Maggie."

"We'll have to write a new one then with eh-yah, da, and mam in it."

"How many people live there?"

"In the privy?"

"No, Maggie, in your house."

"Twelve right now."

"Are you all related?"

"Yes, except for the servants."

"You have servants?"

"Eh-yah. We need them to keep the silver and crystal polished."

"Really?"

"No, Charlotte. I was kidding."

"Twelve you said. Six children and your mother and father. That's only eight. Who are the other four? And don't tell me they're servants."

"My uncle Pat and his wife just came over."

"Over from where?"

"From Timbuktu."

"Really?"

"No, Charlotte, from Ireland. They're staying with us until they can get a place. And they've got twin boys, Michael and Patrick Junior. They're only two months old, so they don't take up much room—yet."

"It must be a lot of work for your mother."

"Oh, everybody pitches in. We make do."

"Does your father have a job?"

"He does. And so do all us kids. Except the twins."

"Really? What kind of jobs?"

"The oldest ones work in the factories. The rest of us peddle papers, pick up coal by the tracks, and sell what we don't use. Deliver milk. Run errands. Whatever we can. Got to earn our keep, Mam says."

❧

An errand to Clark's Dry Goods was nowhere near as much fun as a trip to the yard goods store, Charlotte thought as she walked toward the shop on Elm Street. For one thing, Mrs. Clark was usually behind the counter, and Charlotte was afraid of her. It wasn't that Mrs. Clark had ever said anything mean. Actually Charlotte had never heard her say anything at all except the amount of money something cost, but Mrs. Clark was scary because one of her eyes looked in one direction and the other eye moved around a lot. That was unsettling. Other than Mrs. Clark's eyes, there was nothing interesting in this store: just bags and barrels of flour, salt, barley, and such.

"Two pounds of barley, please," Charlotte said. She wished she knew which of Mrs. Clark's eyes was seeing her. Maybe they both were. Maybe Mrs. Clark got two different views of everything. Charlotte tried to imagine how that would be. Mrs. Clark nodded and took a two-pound sack from the counter and the scoop from the top of the barrel. She placed the sack on the scale.

"Twenty-five cents," she said, handing the filled sack to Charlotte.

As Charlotte left the dry goods shop, she realized that she was very near the corner of Meadow Street. As she headed for home she thought about Maggie's house on Meadow Street. Imagine all those about people working, breathing, eating, and sleeping in one house.

She thought she'd like to see Maggie's house. Maggie knew where Charlotte lived, but Charlotte had never even been down Meadow Street. *Well, why not do it now?* Aunt Lucy was going to be at the temperance meeting this afternoon, so she wouldn't be worrying. Charlotte could walk back to the corner of Elm and Meadow, turn right down Meadow to Main Street, and then down Broad. It would be the long way home, to be sure, but not that far. She wouldn't stop, of course, but she'd see Maggie's house and neighborhood. Maybe Maggie would see her walking by. Wouldn't she be surprised! She imagined Maggie running out to hug her and then insisting, over Charlotte's protests, on taking her in to meet the family. Charlotte turned around and headed back to Meadow Street.

She was glad she had only an arithmetic book to carry home today. She tucked the barley bag under her right arm, her book under her left. As soon as she turned the corner, the shops gave way to houses—narrow, two-story houses packed side by side on both sides of the street with almost no land between them. More of them were gray than any other color, so Charlotte couldn't tell which one was Maggie's. Laundry hung on lines suspended from the second story of many of the houses. It was different at her house. Bridget would have hung the Hulls' laundry in the clothes yard, where clothesline ran back and forth between the two clothes poles. There were children playing in front of a gray house, but they were little ones who paid no attention to Charlotte as she walked along.

If she lived in the house next door to Maggie,

Charlotte thought, they'd be able to talk to each other without even leaving their houses, just by opening the windows. That would be nice, but there was not a single tree anywhere. She stopped and turned all the way around. She could see the tops of trees over on Elm Street but no others. How could people live without trees? She would miss the trees if she lived next door to Maggie.

Charlotte turned back to go on with her walk and nearly bumped into two boys.

"Oh," she said, "excuse me." She tried to step around them, but they moved to block her way.

The taller of the two boys said, "Look what the pigs dragged over."

"What do you want?" asked the other. "Yankees got no business here."

How did they know she was a Yankee? "I . . . I was just taking a w-w-walk," Charlotte whispered.

The shorter one snickered. "A w-w-walk? What's in that sack?" He reached for it.

"B-b-barley," Charlotte said, pulling the bag back out of reach, "for my aunt."

"B-b-barley!" the shorter one mocked. "Yankees sure talk funny."

He yanked the sack from her and peered in.

"Look, Kevin, a gift from a Yank. She wants us to have some b-b-barley."

"Oh, please don't take it," Charlotte said. "I'll go. Please give it back."

"You'll want to be giving that back now," said a voice from behind Charlotte. Charlotte turned to see a very fat man with a long, red beard. He spoke to the boy holding the sack.

"Give it back nothing!" the bigger boy said. "Don't give it to her, Shawn. It's ours now. She wants us to have it."

The man stepped around Charlotte to grab each boy by the arm. "And now she wants it back," he said as he turned them all the way around to face Charlotte again. "So, you'll kindly give it back and wish the young lady a pleasant walk."

"Ow!" one boy said. Both boys had pained expressions on their faces as the man spoke again to the boy with the sack. "You'll be wanting to give it back right now, I think," he said.

The boy thrust it back toward Charlotte, who grabbed it.

"Thank you so much," she said. "I was just—"

"We'll just stand right here and wish you good

luck on your way," said the bearded man. "Best you hurry along now."

Charlotte didn't stop running until she had turned the corner onto Main Street.

4

Bruises

*H*eard you had a bad time yesterday."

"I just wanted to see where you live, Maggie. Do you know the man who helped me?"

"Jack O'Malley."

"He was very nice."

"He gave those boys what for, I'll tell you."

"I didn't mean to get anyone in trouble, Maggie."

"Those two are always in trouble, Charlotte. I was working in the kitchen and missed all the excitement. I suppose rich kids like you and Zach just sit around the house after school letting Bridget wait on you."

"Oh, no. I help with the cooking and the doing up and run errands. That's where I'd been yesterday—at the dry goods for my aunt."

"So what does Zach do?"

"He brings in wood and helps out in the yard. On Saturdays he works for my uncle at the factory."

"Zach works at the whip factory?"

"Eh-yah. He just started this summer."

"Are there any poor Yankees?"

"Of course there are. Zach and I are poor."

"Charlotte, look where you live. Look how you dress. You're not poor."

"That's Uncle Hiram and Aunt Lucy's money. Not ours. My uncle makes Zach put the money he earns in the bank."

"In the bank. Think of that."

"Do your parents know we're friends?"

"No. Do your aunt and uncle know?"

"My aunt would kill me."

"Ah, best we prevent bloodshed then. And best you stay away from Meadow Street, Charlotte.

There's some don't think much of Yanks.

"*Why?*"

"*I don't know. But things are bad, and they're getting worse.*"

"*Eh-yah.*"

❧

The carriage was in front of the house when Charlotte got home from school. Regal's reins were loosely wrapped around the hitching post. Charlotte took a moment to stroke the horse's nose. Regal snorted with pleasure and bobbed his head. She gave a quick wave to the statues and ran up the steps, reaching for the doorknob just as the door was pulled open.

"Oh!" Charlotte stepped back in surprise. "Aunt Lucy!"

Her aunt had on her best walking dress of light tan brocaded silk with matching broad-brimmed hat, the feathers curling around the crown. Her black velvet cape was over her arm.

"Fancy meeting you here, Charlotte," she said. For a moment, Charlotte was puzzled. Wasn't she supposed to be here? Where else would she be? But Aunt Lucy was smiling. She was joking. Charlotte smiled.

Aunt Lucy said, "You're in charge of supper tonight. I left a meatloaf ready for the oven. Put some potatoes and carrots in with it. That'll do. Oh, and the turnips are in the sack just inside the cellar door. Bridget made Indian pudding for dessert."

"Aren't you eating?"

"I'll eat when I get home."

"Where are you going?"

"Emergency Anti-Slavery Society meeting. They are going to march poor Frederick Burns through the streets of Boston and then return him to his owner. Imagine getting all this way, going through all he went through, and then, because of the Fugitive Slave Law, being humiliated and sent back. It's inhuman!"

"The Anti-Slavery Society is marching him through the streets?"

"No, no. The authorities in Boston. We've got to send representatives to Boston immediately. That's why we're meeting midmonth. I should be home around eight." Mrs. Hull put on her cape as she went down the steps and took the reins from the hitching post. She stepped up on the cement mount at the side of the street and then into the driver's seat. She clicked her tongue, and Regal began a slow trot up the street.

Charlotte took down one of the aprons hanging on the kitchen door, tied it at her neck and waist, and brought the meatloaf out of the icebox. She thought about runaway slaves as she cleaned three large potatoes under the sink pump. Aunt Lucy was reading aloud each chapter of *Uncle Tom's Cabin* as it appeared in the paper. Hearing about Eliza running away with her son, Harry, and Uncle Tom being tortured by his owner, the terrible Simon Legree, had made Charlotte think a lot about slavery. She tried to imagine what it must be like to be owned by someone. Even she could not imagine it. She certainly hoped Aunt Lucy's group and others like it would put a stop to it soon.

There were ink smudges on her hands, and she scrubbed at them a bit. The carrots were already peeled. She grabbed some purple-topped turnips from the sack and pared and sliced them. She put the turnips in a kettle, pumped water into it at the sink, and lifted the stove lid. The fire was too low for cooking, and the wood box by the stove was empty except for a few kindling scraps and last night's newspaper.

Charlotte went to the foot of the stairs. "Zach!" she called. "Zach!"

She climbed the stairs and knocked on his closed door.

"Zach?"

She was about to turn away when she heard a muffled sound. Opening the door, she saw her brother sitting on the edge of the bed, his head in his hands.

"Zach," she said. "Didn't you hear me calling? We need more wood brought in."

"All right. Give me a minute." His voice was muffled as he spoke through his hands. "Has Aunt Lucy gone?"

"Yes. And I'm supposed to fix supper, but we need wood."

Zachary said nothing.

"Zach? What's the matter with you? Are you sick?" She walked over to him.

He lifted his face and turned toward her.

"Zach! What's happened? What did you do to your face?" Charlotte reached out and then drew back as he winced.

"How bad is it?"

"Well, it's a mess. Wait." Charlotte ran into her

room, grabbed a hand mirror from the dresser, and went back to Zach. "Look at yourself."

Zachary held the mirror in one hand while he gingerly touched several spots on his face. "Ohhh," he moaned. "Do you think it'll look all right by tomorrow?"

"By tomorrow? By next month, maybe." Charlotte poured water into a bowl from the pitcher under his window. "Here. Wash yourself. I'll get some ice." She ran down to the kitchen and pumped water over a washrag. She put that down on the kitchen table, opened the icebox, and grabbed the pick. She used it to jab the ice cake until a good-size piece fell off. She hurried back to her brother's room, wrapping the ice with the washrag on the way.

He was dabbing gently at his face with a towel. He turned to face her. "How do I look?"

"Well, with some of the grime and blood washed off, you look a little better, but that eye's turning black. The cut near your ear isn't much, but your lip's pretty swollen." Charlotte said. "Let me put some ice on it. What happened?" she asked again.

"What do you suppose happened?" he asked. "A fight."

"Who with?"

"Just some boys."

"Why did you fight them?"

"They jumped us."

"Jumped who?"

"Whit and me. We were just walking home from school, minding our own business, and they jumped us. We gave as good as we got, though." He nodded with satisfaction and tried to smile, then winced.

"Eh-yah. I'll bet. How many were there?" Charlotte asked.

"Just two. But they were big. Lots bigger than us. You know how big those Irish kids get." Zach took the ice from her and touched it to his lip.

"How could you tell they were Irish?" Charlotte asked.

"Charlotte, they were Irish."

"And they jumped you for no reason?"

"I'd never even seen them before."

"What about Whit? Did he know them?"

"I think so."

"Who stopped the fight?"

"I don't know. It just stopped. We all got up and—"

A door slammed downstairs.

"Anybody home?"

Charlotte raised her eyebrows at Zach, who motioned her away.

She ran down the stairs. "Welcome home, Uncle Hiram," she said, hugging him. He always smelled so good: part leather from the factory, part shaving cream, part an unidentifiable something that she never smelled anywhere else. She rubbed her cheek against the rough wool of his suit.

He took her by the shoulders and kissed the top of her head. "Thank you, Peanut. Where's Zach?"

"Oh, he'll be down in a minute. Supper will be a little late. I've got to get more wood."

"Let Zachary bring in the wood," her uncle said.

"That's all right," Charlotte said as she opened the back door. "I don't mind."

Her uncle hung his coat and hat on the hall tree, picked up the newspaper, and went into the front room, taking his pipe from the rack as he passed. Charlotte was still at work in the kitchen when she heard Zachary's slow step on the stairs and then Uncle Hiram's voice: "Well, Zach. How does the other fellow look?"

5

Evenings Out

*D*o your brothers fight?"

"All the time. Does Zach?"

"He got hurt in one."

"Who with?"

"Some Irish boys, he said. Why do your brothers fight?"

"Why is the sky blue?"

"What does the sky have to do with it?"

"Nothing, Charlotte. I just meant that they fight because they're boys. It doesn't matter what the occasion is. My brothers will fight over the time of day."

"You never see girls fighting."

"Not with fists anyway."

"Well, I wish they'd stop it."

"Wishing doesn't solve much, does it?"

"No, I suppose it doesn't. Is your family reading Uncle Tom's Cabin?"

"No one's got time for reading much. There's always work to be done. Da reads the papers."

"Well, it's in the newspaper. There's a new chapter every month. It's all about slaves. It's really good, Maggie."

"Da says we're going to have a war."

"He does? Between the Irish and the Yankees?"

"No. North against South."

"They can't fight a war. They're part of the same country."

"So they say."

"What would they fight about?"

"Slaves and cotton, my da says."

"Oh, Aunt Lucy's Anti-Slavery Society is working on that. There won't have to be a war."

"I'll tell Da. He'll be relieved."

"I wish we could be partners for geography."

"That'd be nice. Who'd you get?"

"Ann Turner. And she hates me. Who did you get?"

"Mike O'Neill."

"I'm going to ask Miss Avery if we can switch."

"Not much chance of that."

"Why not?"

"She's not going to put a Yankee with an Irish, Charlotte. Not if she can help it."

"Why would she care?"

"Why is the sky blue?"

❧

"Where are you going, Zach?" Aunt Lucy asked after supper as Zach took his coat and opened the back door.

"To the Academy," he said, putting on his cap.

"Mr. Allston's astronomy class."

"It's a school night," Aunt Lucy reminded him.

"I'm going to read the next installment of *Uncle Tom's Cabin*. It's episode twenty-five."

"Oh!" Charlotte exclaimed. "I hope we find out about—"

"Who cares?" Zach interrupted. "It's got nothing to do with me."

"Slavery is everybody's concern," Aunt Lucy

insisted. "It must be stopped, and it may be up to you young people to do that."

"Well, not tonight," he said as he headed for the door.

"You come straight home after class. Your uncle is working late. He'll be upset if he gets home before you do." Aunt Lucy picked up a dish and went into the kitchen.

Zach made a face Aunt Lucy didn't see and went out the door.

Although Charlotte was looking forward to the next chapter of the story, she envied Zach on nights like this. *It must be such fun being able to go out after dark. And just imagine looking up at the sky and learning about the stars together. Studies at the Academy must be so much better than at the Green District School, where you learned everything sitting at a desk.*

"Did you go to the Academy, Aunt Lucy?" she asked as they were doing the dishes.

"No," Aunt Lucy said. She swished the soap bar around in the dishwater. "My family moved here when I was twenty-one. Much too old for the Academy."

"How far did you go in school?" Charlotte asked.

"Eighth grade," her aunt answered. "Very few girls went on then. Not like now, when lots of them do."

"Were you poor?"

"We didn't have much," Aunt Lucy said. "I'll tell you that."

"Did you want to go on?"

"Probably." Aunt Lucy rinsed the platter and put it on the sink shelf for Charlotte to dry. "But my folks needed the money, so I went to work in the shoe factory with my father and your father."

"What was my father like?" Charlotte asked.

"When he was a boy, you mean?"

Charlotte nodded.

"Your father was fun. He could mimic anything: birds, animals—people, even. He loved to sing and had a lovely voice. We sang a lot at home."

"He sang? I wonder if he ever sang to me." She was ashamed to admit that she was beginning to forget what both her parents were like.

"I don't know, dear. Probably he did. But when things get hard, we sometimes forget how to sing."

"Were times hard for my mother and father?" Charlotte wanted to know. She was hungry for anything that would help her fill in those fading faces.

"Yes. I think they were."

"Even when they grew up?"

"Even when they grew up."

"Did he like working in the shoe factory when he was a boy?" Charlotte asked.

Aunt Lucy shrugged. "I don't know. I never asked him."

"Did you like it?"

"Working in the factory?" Aunt Lucy put more plates into the dishwater.

Charlotte nodded.

"No," Aunt Lucy said. "It was noisy and dirty, and I hated almost every minute I was there."

"What would you rather have done?" Charlotte dipped a glass in the rinse water and began drying it.

"Oh, I don't know," Aunt Lucy said. She paused a minute before putting a plate in the rinse water. "You do what you have to do. Things worked out for the best." She went on in a different tone of voice. "That's where I met your uncle."

"He worked in the shoe factory?"

Aunt Lucy nodded. "He was one of the bosses."

"And you were on the line?" Charlotte was grinning. She loved hearing stories like this.

Aunt Lucy nodded, her eyes twinkling.

"And?" Charlotte prodded. "And?"

"And what?" Aunt Lucy asked.

"And what happened?"

"And he asked if he could pay a call some evening," she said.

"And you said yes, and you lived happily ever after."

Aunt Lucy smiled. "I said yes, and my father said no. The happy-ever-after part came later."

"Why did your father say no? Didn't he like Uncle Hiram?"

"He didn't know him, Charlotte. He only knew that Hiram was a boss, and I was a worker. He thought your uncle was toying with me."

"But then he got to know Uncle Hiram, and he changed his mind," Charlotte said with a smile.

Aunt Lucy shook her head. "Then I got to know

him. We ran away and got married, and my father had no say in the matter."

"You ran away! Oh, how romantic! Then what happened?"

Aunt Lucy took the dishpan out the back door to dump it. She was smiling when she came back in. "Then things got better. Come on, Charlotte, let's see how Little Eva and Uncle Tom are doing," Aunt Lucy had just picked up the book when the front door opened. "Have I missed much?" Uncle Hiram asked.

"Just about to start," she said.

"Where's Zach?"

"Astronomy class," Charlotte offered.

"What time did he leave?" Uncle Hiram wanted to know.

"Only about a half-hour ago, dear," his wife answered.

ॐ

Charlotte was wakened in the night by loud voices downstairs.

She opened her bedroom door to hear Uncle Hiram saying, "It's midnight, Zach. Where were you?"

"At astronomy class. I told Aunt Lucy."

"Not till this hour, Zach."

"Well, some of the guys and I stayed around to talk. We lost track of time."

"Go to bed. But this doesn't go on, Zach."

Charlotte closed her door before Zach climbed the stairs.

6

Whose Fault?

"Are you going to the bonfire, Maggie?"

"The one in Park Square?"

"Is there another?"

"We have one up on Prospect Hill."

"You do?"

"We do."

"An Irish bonfire?"

"Imagine us knowing how."

"The same night?"

"The same night."

"Why don't you come to the one in Park Square?"

"Because it's a Yankee fire."

"Aren't all bonfires the same?"

"Not the crowd around it."

"What does that matter? Zach says this year's will be bigger than ever. You should come to ours."

"Where is Zach?"

"At the Academy."

"He's older than you?"

"Fourteen."

"What's he like?"

"He's tall, and he has brown hair."

"That's what he looks like. What's he like?"

"Oh, let's see. He likes roast beef and apple pie and—"

"Charlotte, I mean what kind of a person is Zach?"

"I know, Maggie. I was joking."

"You were?"

"I was."

"Imagine that. Does he daydream like you do?"

"Daydream? Zach? No, I never caught him daydreaming."

"Is he as smart in school as you are?"

"Oh, he's very smart. He's studying astronomy. I'd like to learn all about the stars, but he also has to take Greek and Latin, Maggie. That sounds really hard."

"It does that."

"Do you think we'll have trouble with those things?"

"You plan to go to the Academy, Charlotte?"

"Yes. Don't you?"

"We'll see how the money is by then."

"Oh, I hope you go, Maggie. We can help each other study."

"I don't think you'll ever have trouble learning anything at school, Charlotte. Look at how fast you figured out long division. You got the answers before Miss Avery did. Does Zach have a lot of friends?"

"He has a friend named Whit."

"What a funny name."

"Whit told Zach you bought land on Bartlett Street."

"I did?"

"Not you, silly. You Irish."

"Ah. We Irish are at it again, are we? Do you know a Mr. Fowler, Charlotte?"

"There are lots of Fowlers. Which one do you mean?"

"Mr. Samuel Fowler."

"Eh-yah. He lives on West Silver Street. My aunt and his wife are good friends."

"He gave us the land."

"What land?"

"The land on Mechanic Street."

"The empty lot on the corner of Bartlett?"

"Aye."

"He never."

"He did. Guess you Yankees aren't all as tight as ticks."

"It wasn't his land to give, Maggie. It's my uncle's land."

"Not anymore, Charlotte."

❧

Zachary was already seated at breakfast when Charlotte came downstairs the next morning. Charlotte could tell when she went in for breakfast that her aunt and uncle had been arguing. To Charlotte's surprise, Zach didn't seem to be the problem this time.

"Good morning," Aunt Lucy and Uncle Hiram

spoke almost in unison, but neither of them smiled. Zach murmured something without looking up.

Charlotte said, "Good morning," and went around the table to kiss her aunt's and uncle's cheeks before sitting down at her place. Bridget put a plate of ham and eggs in front of her. Charlotte took her napkin from its ring, put it in her lap, and began to eat.

"Why on earth did you sell it to them?" Aunt Lucy said, turning to her husband.

Their breakfast finished, Charlotte's aunt and uncle had pushed their empty plates aside and were facing each other across the table.

"I sold it to Sam Fowler, Lucy," Uncle Hiram said.

"And he turned right around and gave it to the Irish. For a church, of all things. What was he thinking? What were you thinking?"

Bridget came in and removed their plates.

Uncle Hiram waited until Bridget was back in the kitchen. "It was his to do with as he liked, Lucy. Sam made a good offer, and I took it. It was part of my father's estate; we were never going to use it. When business picks up a bit more, I'll put in a new line at the factory, and the money will come in handy."

"You could have stopped it. Sam wouldn't have given it to the Irish if you told him not to."

"Perhaps not."

"I tell you, they're moving in everywhere, Hiram. Eunice Noble says one of them bought a house on Franklin Street. Now think of that. An Irish family on Franklin Street." Aunt Lucy's voice was rising with each new statement. "Right next door to the Chapmans."

Zach looked up quickly, and Charlotte glanced at him and tried not to smile. His lip was no longer swollen, but his black eye had faded to a strange purply yellow. He reminded her of a clown at the circus. He looked hard at Charlotte and then quickly down again.

"I think Franklin Street and the Chapmans will stand the shock, Lucy," Uncle Hiram said.

"It won't stop at one, Hiram. The others won't be far behind. They live three and four families to a house. Heaven knows how many will be moving in. That beautiful Hayes house. Mr. Hayes must be turning over in his grave."

Charlotte pictured a body deep in the ground turning over and over, the headstone on top of the grave bobbing up and down as if a mole were tunneling beneath the surface. She giggled at the thought.

"What's funny, Charlotte?" her uncle asked.

"She's laughing at me!" Zach exclaimed. "Make her stop."

"I'm not," she protested. "I just hiccuped." It would be too hard to explain about the gravestone.

"Take a drink of water," her aunt suggested.

"Next thing you know the Irish will be joining your temperance club, Lucy," Uncle Hiram said as he passed Charlotte the water pitcher.

"Don't stand on one foot until that happens, Hiram."

"Things are changing, Lucy, and we'd all better get used to it. The Irish are here. More are coming because of the potato famine in Ireland. It's time we Yankees let down some barriers."

Zach looked up again. "This!" he exclaimed pointing at his eye. "This is what happens when you're nice to the Irish."

"Oh," Charlotte said. "Were you being nice to

them? I thought you said they jumped you when you were just walking by."

"You know what I mean," Zach said.

"No," Charlotte said. "I think I don't know at all what you mean." She was startled to hear herself speaking up to Zachary that way.

He looked at her now with such anger that she turned quickly away.

Bridget came back into the dining room to remove the plates, and Zach got up from the table.

"Thank you, Bridget," Charlotte said. "That was very good."

Bridget looked up. For a moment she and Charlotte just stared at each other. Then Bridget nodded and returned to the kitchen.

Anxious to forget Zach's angry look, Charlotte worked on building the mental image of her uncle standing on one foot, struggling for balance as Irish women lined up to join the temperance club. That and Mr. Hayes revolving in his grave occupied Charlotte's mind as she walked to school.

Loud shouts destroyed that image. Joining the circle of children by the schoolyard fence, Charlotte could see Jimmy Murphy on the ground with Zenas Clark on top of him. Several of the girls were crying. Others joined the boys in shouting words of encouragement to either Jimmy or Zenas. This was more than the usual tussle. Blood was already running from a cut on Jimmy's forehead as Zenas punched him hard in the jaw.

Charlotte looked around for Maggie, but she was nowhere in sight. Charlotte ran across the playground in search of a teacher. Miss Avery was over by the door, facing away from the fight.

"Miss Avery! Come quickly! A fight! They're fighting!" Charlotte exclaimed.

Maureen O'Neill and Jean Murphy had joined Charlotte now. Jean was crying.

"Oh, hurry," Jean sobbed. "My brother's really hurt! Zenas is killing him!"

Slowly, much too slowly, it seemed to Charlotte, Miss Avery turned and began to walk toward the fight.

"Hurry! They're fighting!" Charlotte said again as she and the other girls ran a few steps toward the fight and then back to the teacher, urging her on. If Charlotte had dared, she'd have grabbed Miss Avery's hand and dragged her across the playground.

Even when Miss Avery finally got to the ring of

children circling the fight, she paused. Why didn't she push them aside and stop the fight? Jimmy was still on the ground, blood now smeared all over his face.

Then Jimmy pulled his knees to his chest and, placing his feet on Zenas's chest, shoved hard. Some in the crowd cheered, and others booed as Zenas fell back. Jimmy, regaining his footing, jumped on top of Zenas and began hitting him in the face.

"Here! Here! What's all this?" Miss Avery said, stepping into the circle at last. She yanked Jimmy off Zenas, took the boys by the shoulders, and turned to the crowd. "Go about your business," she said. "Fight's over. You boys come with me. Shame on you, James."

Shame on James? The fight must have been his fault. But how would Miss Avery have known that? Maybe someone had told her.

༚

It was soft voices that Charlotte heard outside her bedroom door that night.

"Zachary." It was Aunt Lucy's voice. "What's wrong with you?"

"Wrong with me?" Zach whispered, but Charlotte could hear the anger. "Nothing's wrong with me. I'm tired. That's all."

"Do you need help with your studies? Because your uncle—"

"I don't need Uncle Hiram showing how smart he is. I'm not dumb. If I didn't have all this other work here and at the factory, I'd have no trouble keeping up with the Irish or anyone else."

"I know it's hard, Zach," Aunt Lucy said.

"Why do I have to work at the factory? Don't you have enough money?"

"It isn't the money, Zach. You know that. The money you earn will be yours when you need it. Uncle Hiram wants you to know what that kind of labor is like. He worked on the line, and so did I. Someday you'll be running the factory and—"

"What if I don't want to run the dumb factory? What if I just don't want to?" Zach was no longer trying to keep his voice down.

"Then you'll do something else." Uncle Hiram's voice cut in. Every word sliced the air. "But you'll know what hard labor is. Now go to bed. It's late."

Two doors closed—one gently and one with a slam.

7
Vandalism

I hate the way things are now, Maggie."

"*Which things?*"

"The fighting. The arguing. Everybody seems mad all the time. I wish it was like it used to be."

"*How did it used to be?*"

"Oh, you know. People used to be nice to each other."

"*I see. Like Ann and her group were?*"

"Well, that was just to me. Why do they hate me so, Maggie?"

"Ann's a bully. She probably doesn't know why she picked you, and the others follow like sheep."

"Well, now everybody's being nasty and saying mean things."

"Da says the newspapers aren't helping much."

"They aren't? What are they saying?"

"They print a lot about the Know-Nothings."

"What a funny name! Who are they?"

"Politicians, I think."

"Do they really know nothing? And if they do, why are they letting people know that they know nothing?"

"They know that they want no Catholics in the country."

"No Catholics? You mean no Irish?"

"There's other Catholics besides us, Charlotte. There's Polish and German and French and Italian Catholics."

"But we don't have any of those other people."

"Not in Westfield, but in Springfield and Chicopee and all around there are lots of immigrants. I don't know why there's only Irish and Yankees in Westfield."

"And the Know-Nothings want to get rid of you all?"

"They do."

"Why?"

"I don't know, Charlotte."

"I'm glad we don't fight, Maggie."

"Me, too. Your turn."

❧

They were just finishing supper when Uncle Hiram said, "Sam Fowler's house was broken into last night. I thought we'd go over later."

"Broken into?" Aunt Lucy exclaimed. "The Fowlers? Why didn't you tell me? We should have gone right away. Was anyone hurt?"

"No. He and Lydia were over at the Bridgmans'. They didn't get home until nearly midnight, and the culprits were long gone."

"Did they get away with much?" Aunt Lucy asked.

"Sam says not," Uncle Hiram said. "They did a bit of damage, though."

Aunt Lucy stood up. "If there's much damage, there'll be plenty of cleaning up to do. Such a thing. And to Sam and Lydia Fowler! Why would the Irish do them harm? Sam gave them the land, for goodness' sake."

"What makes you think it's the Irish, Lucy?" Uncle Hiram asked as he stood and pushed in his chair.

"Who else?" she asked. "It's always the Irish. No Yankee would do harm to another."

"Somebody's got to stop those Irish," Zach said. "You should see how it is at the Academy. The Irish are always trying to make us look bad."

"Lucy," Uncle Hiram said, ignoring Zach's comment, "just take a look at our history. You can't say that Yankees never harm Yankees."

"Well, we never had trouble here before the Irish came."

Uncle Hiram laughed. "That's quite a memory you have, my dear. Let's see. The first of the Irish came to build the canal. That would have been 1838. Your folks came here in 1842. Do tell us about life in Westfield before the Irish came, Lucy."

"There's no need to be sarcastic, Hiram." Aunt Lucy began to clear the table.

"Has it always been this way?" Charlotte asked as she picked up a platter.

"What way, dear?" Aunt Lucy asked. "Zach, clear those crumbs from your place, please."

"All this fighting between the Yankees and the Irish," Charlotte said.

"No," Uncle Hiram said. "We needed a canal, but nobody wanted to pick up a shovel and start digging. We were begging for workers then. The Irish came ready and willing to do the jobs nobody else wanted to do. The canal never amounted to anything." He took his coat and hat from the hall tree. "But track needed laying for the railroad, and there were still jobs aplenty. The Irish laid the track and were glad of the work. The railroad's done. Times are harder now. Jobs are hard to come by. People get scared when there's not enough work, and they start looking around for someone to blame. And then there's the school. You know this is the first time Irish and Yankee kids have been together in school."

"And they're all over the Academy," Zach said.

"Six Irish boys and one Irish girl," Charlotte reminded him. "All over?"

"Well, there ought not to be any," Zach growled.

"What's her name?" Charlotte asked.

"Whose name?" Zach demanded.

"The Irish girl at the Academy," Charlotte said.

"Who knows?" Zach said. "Who cares?"

"Well, I'm sure her friends do," Charlotte said.

"Friends!" Zach snorted. "She doesn't have any friends. Not at school anyway."

"Then she must be very lonely," Charlotte said softly.

"She should have stayed where she—" Zach began.

Aunt Lucy interrupted. "No time for arguments. Put those dishes in the kitchen, and we'll do them up when we get back from the Fowlers'." She walked quickly to the hall tree and took down her shawl. She turned back to the others. "Charlotte, bring the squash pie. Poor Lydia. She must be beside herself."

"But that's our dessert," Zach protested.

Uncle Hiram turned to stare at his nephew.

"Sorry," Zachary said.

There was a line of carriages outside the Fowlers' house. Uncle Hiram joined a group of men standing at the bottom of the front steps. Charlotte and Aunt Lucy hurried inside as Zach walked toward a group of boys sweeping up glass near the back door.

Mrs. Fowler was seated in the front room while

women and girls went from carriages to the kitchen, bringing in food.

"Come in, Lucy. And Charlotte. So good of you to come," Mrs. Fowler said, starting to rise from her chair.

"Oh, don't get up. What can we do to help?" Aunt Lucy asked. She leaned down to kiss her friend's cheek.

"Mrs. Fowler," Charlotte said, "I'm so sorry."

"Thank you, child," Mrs. Fowler said. "And how kind of you to bring the pie. It looks delicious. There's really no need for all this. Most of the damage was to the back door and windows. They did get into the root cellar and broke most of the jars of food there, but Sam's already replaced the windows, and the boys are cleaning up."

"We laid up much more than I'm going to need this winter," Aunt Lucy said. "I'll send Zach over with some of that blueberry jam and some of the beans, too."

"I've more than enough carrots and beets," Mrs. Turner said. "Among us, we've got plenty to see you through. But what an awful thing. Who would do such a thing?"

"Just boys out for devilry, I expect," Mrs. Fowler said. "Everybody's been so kind and helpful. I've done nothing, really, but sit here and act like the Queen of Sheba. Charlotte, do take that lovely pie into the kitchen and help yourself to some of the food people brought. This is turning into a party, I think. And go find the other girls. They're on the side porch. Tell them to come inside where it's warm."

Charlotte had no intention of joining the girls. She took a piece of salt pork cake from one of the many platters of food in the kitchen and went back into the front hallway. By standing just to the left of the door, she could overhear what the ladies said, and, as the door opened to admit more arrivals, she could hear snatches of conversation from the men on the steps.

"Sam, any idea who did this?" That was Uncle Hiram's voice.

"No, just kids, I suppose. Up to no good."

The door swung shut, and Charlotte's attention went back to the ladies in the living room.

"Bold as you please," someone was saying. "With her ankles right out there for the world to see."

"Not a bit of modesty in the whole bunch of them," another said.

"I think they show much more than their ankles at the tavern."

The door opened to admit Mr. and Mrs. Carpenter. Charlotte stepped back into the shadows as they went by.

"Don't be so sure," one of the men on the front steps said. "It may not be the Irish. Some folks don't like what's been going on in Westfield. Giving the Micks your land was just asking for trouble."

A different voice said, "Aye, and folks think hard of all those Irish you've been hiring, Hiram."

The door closed.

In the parlor, talk had turned to dress patterns. Charlotte was glad when the outside door opened to admit the Walker family and she could hear the men again. Their voices were getting louder.

"Keep 'em in their place. That's the thing."

"Makin' Yankees answer to the Micks."

"Devil worshipers. That's what they are."

"Best watch yourself and think again about what you're doing," a man called out.

From her listening post in the darkness of the

hallway, Charlotte drew in a breath. This fight of words was almost as frightening as the fistfight on the playground.

"Take it for what it's worth."

"It's not worth the gunpowder to blow it to smithereens." Her uncle's voice was angry. "Charlotte, go fetch your aunt. There's nothing more to be done here."

As she turned to get her aunt, Charlotte realized that Uncle Hiram must have known she was there the whole time.

8

The Trick

*M*y brother Michael knows Zach."

"*Really? Are they friends?*"

"*I don't think so. He knows him from the factory.*"

"*Michael works at my uncle's factory?*"

"*He does.*"

"*On Saturdays?*"

"*And Mondays, and Tuesdays and Wednesdays and—*"

"*How old is Michael?*"

"Thirteen."

"How long has he worked there?"

"Couple of years."

"Does he like it?"

"He brings in more money than anybody else except my father."

"Wouldn't he rather go to school?"

"Never asked him."

"Do any of the rest of your family work in my uncle's factory?"

"My father does. And my uncle Pat's just been hired."

"Your father? Is your father Mike Nolan?"

"He is."

"My uncle says he's a good man."

"He is that."

"Uncle Hiram wants to make him foreman, but my aunt's afraid there'll be trouble if he does."

"He did. Two weeks ago."

"Oh. Do you think there will be trouble, Maggie?"

"The Irish are no strangers to trouble, Charlotte."

"Does your father like being foreman?"

"The money's better. We may be able to go shares on a horse."

"You don't have a horse?"

"We don't."

"Then how do you get places?"

"Shank's mare."

"You walk everywhere?"

"When we don't run."

"Where would you go with a horse?"

"We've relatives in Springfield."

"Springfield's not far."

"It is on shank's mare."

❧

Charlotte came downstairs on Saturday morning to find Zachary and her uncle glowering at each other across the breakfast table.

"It's not a matter of choice, Zach," her uncle said after a brief nod to Charlotte as she kissed his cheek and Aunt Lucy's before she sat down.

Uncle Hiram cleared his throat. "It's your job, Zach. We agreed. A gentleman honors an agreement."

"I never agreed to work for a Mick."

"Maybe you can find another place for Zach

in the factory, Hiram," Aunt Lucy said.

Her husband stood up. "Zach, let's leave the womenfolk to their breakfast in peace. You and I will step outside."

Zach started to protest.

"Outside, Zach," his uncle said. He turned and went out the back door.

For a moment Zach sat with his head down. His aunt reached out a hand toward his clenched fist on the table, but he stood and followed his uncle out the door.

When Zach got home that night, he went straight to his room without speaking, and later he ignored calls to supper.

After a meal during which no one spoke except for saying the grace, Aunt Lucy took a tray from the kitchen, filled a plate with food, put the plate on the tray, and took it up to Zach.

Charlotte knocked on Zach's door on her way to bed.

"What?"

"Can I come in?" She waited.

After a minute he said, "I guess."

Zach was sitting at the table, his arms folded against his chest. Open textbooks surrounded an almost empty plate on the table on which was a small crust of bread. His wastebasket was full of crumpled papers. He glowered at Charlotte as he kicked rhythmically at the table leg. She closed the door and leaned against it.

"What do you want?" he asked.

"I just wanted to say good night," she said. "We don't seem to do anything but argue lately, Zach."

"Good night."

"I'm sorry, Zach."

"What are you sorry about? You didn't do anything, did you?"

"No," she said. "I didn't mean that. I meant I'm sorry you're upset."

"You'd be upset too," he growled, "if you quit your dreaming and looked around you to see what's happening."

"What would I see, Zach?"

"You'd see the Irish taking over everything. You'd see Uncle Hiram not doing anything about it."

"What can he do?"

"He can stop giving them jobs, that's what. And Aunt Lucy! What does she do but go running off to meetings to stop people from having a drink and to interfere with what's going on in other places. She should do something about what's going on here!"

"She's working to free slaves, Zach! Haven't you been listening to the story?"

"Stories! Who cares about made-up stories? Whit says most slaves like being slaves. Most masters are kind to their slaves. Even the Bible says slavery is right. Quit your dreaming, Charlotte. Open your eyes. You and Aunt Lucy get all up in arms over slaves in the South. We're being treated like slaves right here in this house, Charlotte."

"Who? You and me? Slaves?" Charlotte shook her head. "Zach, that's not true."

"It is true," Zach insisted. "We have to do everything Uncle Hiram and Aunt Lucy say to do. We work all the time, and for what?"

"For a place to live," Charlotte said. "A chance to go to school."

"There are plenty of places to live, and school's not everything, you know. If things keep on like this, I'm leaving."

"Leaving? Leaving me? Leaving Aunt Lucy and Uncle Hiram?"

"Yes, I am."

"Where would you go, Zach?"

"I don't know yet. But the money I earn at the factory is in my name as well as Uncle Hiram's. I don't know how much it is, but I'll bet it's a lot."

"How does Whit Warren know so much about slavery?" Charlotte asked. Slavery seemed like a much more comfortable topic than Zach's leaving home.

"Because he's been there, Charlotte. That's why." Zach didn't seem angry so much as exasperated with her.

"Whit Warren has been a slave?" Charlotte asked.

"Of course not," Zach said. "But he's been to Virginia. He's seen lots of slaves. His uncle even owns some."

"And Whit talked to the slaves, and they told Whit they were happy?"

"Oh, go to bed, Charlotte, and quit talking nonsense."

She started for the door and then turned back.

"Zach, do the Irish students at the Academy get along?"

"Get along with who?"

"Are there any fights between the Yankees and the Irish?"

"Fistfights?"

"Eh-yah."

Zach gave a brief snort of laughter. "Not during school. The teachers don't let much happen during school. After school those Irish kids gang up on us, and there are plenty of fights."

"Gang up?" she asked. "How can six Irish boys and a girl gang up?"

"It's not just the ones at the Academy, Charlotte. They've got friends."

He closed his book and stood up. "Whole gangs of Irish kids stand outside the Academy just looking for trouble, and, believe me, they get it. And you be sure to stay away from the Irish at Green District School, Charlotte. They're nothing but trouble."

Charlotte stared at Zach for a long moment. "Good night, Zach," she said finally and went to bed.

ε

It had been raining for several days. When Zach complained about the endless gray and damp,

Aunt Lucy said the Good Lord always filled the wells before He froze the ground. Now there were puddles all over the playground. What little ground showed was very muddy.

A small group had gathered around another fight in the schoolyard when Charlotte arrived. There were fights almost every day now, and no one tried to stop them.

Charlotte looked around for Maggie, who usually got there first. Charlotte stepped carefully around the puddles to reach her usual place by the girls' door and wait. She didn't want to get her shoes any muddier than they already were.

To her surprise Ann Turner and her friends approached with smiles on their faces. Ann had a long rope in her hand.

"Want to play, Charlotte?" she asked.

"Me?"

"Yes, we need a twirler," Molly Dewey said.

"Oh, no, thank you."

"Come on, Charlotte," Ann urged. "Play with us for a change."

"Yes," Molly said. "You never play with us anymore."

"We've missed you," Ann said. "Come on, take

an end." She held out one end of the rope.

"Isn't it too muddy for jump rope?" Charlotte asked.

"Oh, it'll be all right if we're careful," Ann said.

"We'll find a dry spot."

Charlotte looked anxiously from one face to another. They were all smiling. She thought maybe she should accept. Aunt Lucy would be pleased to know that they were playing together. Charlotte looked quickly around. There was still no sign of Maggie.

"Yes, come play with us, Charlotte," Maud Adams urged.

"All right," Charlotte said. She held out her hand for one end of the rope.

"Let's go over there where it's not so muddy," Ann said, pointing to the far corner of the playground.

It looked just as muddy there as everywhere else, but Charlotte was in no position to argue. Ann took the other end of the rope and stood in the corner of the fence facing the playground. Charlotte stepped back with her end, taking care to step around the puddles. The other girls lined up to take their turns.

Charlotte and Ann began to twirl, but suddenly the rope went slack, and Ann ran toward her. As Charlotte blinked in surprise, the other girls grabbed the rope and began to twist it around her. Before she knew what was happening, Charlotte was bound from her shoulders to her ankles. One push from Ann, and Charlotte fell sideways into a puddle. She lay there struggling to get her hands free.

"Play with the Micks and you are a Mick."

"Dirty Mick lover. Dirty Mick," they yelled over their shoulders as they ran away.

"Oh, Charlotte," said a welcome voice, and Maggie bent to untwist the rope. "I'm sorry I was late. The twins were—What have they done?"

Maggie led her over to the pump at the side of the school and held her handkerchief under the waterspout. No one paid any attention. By the time they had taken some of the mud off, Charlotte and Maggie were alone on the playground.

"I thought they really wanted to play with me," Charlotte sniffed. "I should have known better. Why are they so mean? What did I ever do to them?"

Maggie shook her head. "I don't know, Charlotte. We'd better get inside. We're late. Miss Avery will be mad."

The two girls walked together into the classroom. Ann and her friends were all in their seats, looking as if butter wouldn't melt in their mouths. Charlotte glanced down at herself. She was a mess. Her shoes and her dress were covered with mud. She hoped it was all off her face.

"You're late," Miss Avery said.

"I'm sorry, Miss Avery," Maggie said, "but Charlotte fell."

"That's Charlotte's excuse," Miss Avery said. "What's yours, Margaret?"

"I was helping her."

"I'm sure Charlotte is quite capable of picking herself up off the ground," Miss Avery said. "Take your seats, and I'll see you both after school."

"But Miss Avery—" Charlotte began.

"Not another word!" Miss Avery said. "To your seats."

Tears were running down Charlotte's cheeks as she sat. She brushed them away and tried to concentrate on the lessons. After school she would explain to Miss Avery what had happened. She didn't like to be a tattletale, but this was too much. Miss Avery would have to know. Those girls should be punished. Miss Avery would write notes to their parents. They might even be expelled from school. Charlotte pictured them begging for her forgiveness. Would she give it? Not before she'd told them a thing or two.

Usually Charlotte went home for dinner at noon, but Aunt Lucy was going to be at a temperance meeting, and so Charlotte had brought her dinner pail. She ate by herself, standing by the door as usual.

"I'll hurry back," Maggie had said as she headed home.

Most of the children avoided looking directly at Charlotte as they went out to the playground. Charlotte was relieved when, true to her word, Maggie came back quickly.

The afternoon session went by as usual. The dismissal bell rang, and Charlotte and Maggie remained in their seats while the others left. Ann paused to turn to Charlotte and smile as she rubbed one index finger over the other in the sign for shame.

Miss Avery came back in the room. "Take out

your papers, girls, and write 'I will not be late for school' fifty times. And I want each letter perfect."

"Miss Avery," Charlotte said, standing up. "I'd like to explain what happened. This was not our fault."

"Did I ask you for excuses?" Miss Avery asked.

"No, but—"

"Start writing," Miss Avery said, and she left the room. Both girls bent over their tasks.

Charlotte finished first and remained in her seat until Maggie put down her pencil. Miss Avery was back at her desk. When they handed her their papers, she said, "Margaret, you may leave. Charlotte, you may remain here for a moment."

Oh good, Charlotte thought. *She is going to give me a chance to explain. When I do, those girls will really be in for a scolding.* She decided she'd start by explaining how those girls had behaved that awful night when they tore up her pressed-leaf book. That would set the stage for their behavior today as part of a list of mean things they had done. She imagined Miss Avery standing over a tearful Ann and her friends, demanding that they write "I will not be unkind to Charlotte" one thousand times.

"Charlotte," Miss Avery began. "I've been meaning to talk with you. You know that your aunt and uncle hold a position of high esteem in Westfield."

"Yes, Miss Avery," Charlotte said, "but Ann Turner—"

"We are not talking about Ann Turner," Miss Avery interrupted. "We are talking about you, Charlotte, and your unfortunate choice of friends."

"Unfortunate ch . . ." Charlotte stammered. "Well, Ann is not really my friend. You see, her mother and father—"

"I'm talking about Margaret Nolan," Miss Avery said.

"Maggie? Margaret?" This was not going at all the way Charlotte had expected.

"Yes," Miss Avery said. "I realize that your own background is less privileged than some, but even you must realize how very lucky you are to have been taken in by such wonderful people."

"Oh, yes, Miss Avery," Charlotte said quickly. "I know that, but those girls—"

"And, apparently, when some of the girls here very nicely tried to involve you in their games, hoping to persuade you to stay with your own kind, just because you missed, you responded by throwing yourself on the ground in a temper tantrum."

"What?" Charlotte exclaimed. "Temper tantrum? Me? But I didn't—"

"Charlotte," Miss Avery said. "I have spoken to both Ann and Molly. I know what happened. You cannot lie your way out of this."

"But—"

"We'll say no more about this, Charlotte," Miss Avery went on. "I will not tell your aunt and uncle this time, but do not let me hear of any other such behavior on your part. You may not come from quality, but you are surrounded by it now. You owe it to your aunt and uncle to behave in a lady-like manner."

"Miss Avery, please let me—"

"I'll hear no more, Charlotte. Go now."

Charlotte ran all the way home with tears running down her face. She didn't know which betrayal was worse, Ann's or Miss Avery's.

Aunt Lucy was putting wood in the parlor stove when Charlotte burst in the door. "Charlotte, what happened? You're very late. I was worried. And look at you! You're a sight!"

Charlotte said, "I fell."

"Well, go wash yourself up and get changed," Aunt Lucy said.

Charlotte dashed upstairs, threw herself down on the bed and cried.

❧

"Everything all right, Charlotte?" Uncle Hiram asked. They were all seated at the supper table when Charlotte came down.

"Yes," Charlotte said. She sat in her chair, pulled her napkin from its ring, and placed it in her lap.

"Did you hurt yourself when you fell?" Aunt Lucy asked.

"No," Charlotte answered without looking up.

"What happened?" Aunt Lucy pressed.

"Did you get in a fight?" Zach asked. "Was it the Micks? Just tell me which ones and I'll—"

"Zach," her uncle said, "let Charlotte speak."

Charlotte kept her eyes on her lap. Aunt Lucy and Uncle Hiram were friends with the parents of all those girls. They wouldn't believe her any more than Miss Avery did. Charlotte shook her head. "Nothing happened," she said. "I just fell."

For a long moment no one spoke. Charlotte could hear the sound of their silverware on the plates as they ate. She looked at the meat, potatoes, and peas congealing on her own plate. She picked up her fork and then put it down again.

"Charlotte," said Aunt Lucy. "You know you can tell us anything—anything at all."

Charlotte looked from her aunt's face to her uncle's. They had finished eating and were looking at her.

And then, looking down again, she did tell. She told them all about Maggie and the fun they'd had together. She paused and looked up. Nobody spoke. Their expressions told her nothing, so she looked down again before she went on. She told them about the mean trick and the laughter and the mud. Another pause for breath. Another glance around the table and then back to her lap. She told them about Miss Avery and what she had said. This time she didn't want to stop until it was all out.

In the silence that followed, Charlotte continued looking down at her napkin. She'd done it. She'd disgraced them all. Probably Aunt Lucy and Uncle Hiram would not want her to live here anymore.

Where would she go? Would Maggie's parents take her in? Their house was already overcrowded. And besides, she was a Yankee—a Yankee who didn't know her own kind. No one would want her. Aunt Lucy and Uncle Hiram would send her back to Agawam. She'd have to go from house to house, begging people to take her in. Perhaps they'd send her to an orphanage.

When she looked up, her eyes were so full of tears that she couldn't see the expressions on their faces.

Aunt Lucy pushed back her chair and came over to hug Charlotte. "Oh, you poor thing," she said. "I'm going to the school tomorrow. I have a few words to say to Miss Avery."

Charlotte was stunned. "You're not mad? You believe me?"

Uncle Hiram reached across the table and grasped Charlotte's hand. "Of course we believe you, Peanut. I'm glad you have a friend," he said. "Good ones are hard to come by."

"You don't care that she's Irish?" Charlotte looked from her uncle to her aunt.

"Care?" Zach snarled. "Of course we care. You should see what goes on in their church. They pray to statues, and they talk in Latin so no one can understand them. You stay away from them, Charlotte. They'll be after you next."

"Zach, don't be silly," Aunt Lucy began. "After Charlotte? That's ridiculous. And how would you know what goes on in their church?"

Zach squinted up his eyes as he faced his aunt. "I know because Whit's seen it. He peeked in the window and saw it all."

"They haven't even had a Mass there yet," Charlotte said. "How could Whit have seen it?"

"They have this secret ceremony they do in people's houses. I tell you, Whit knows. He told us all about it. They kneel in front of a statue. It's devil worship," Zach insisted.

"Charlotte, were all the Yankee girls in on the trick?" Aunt Lucy said. "Because if—"

"Charlotte," Uncle Hiram interrupted. "We don't care if your friend is Irish. Do we, Lucy?"

"No," his wife said after a brief pause. She nodded as if agreeing with herself. "We don't care."

"But you hate the Irish," Charlotte said.

"We sure do," Zach said. "And if you weren't friends with one—"

"You'd have had to play with those mean girls,"
Aunt Lucy finished.

"That's not what I—" Zach protested.

"We don't hate the Irish," Uncle Hiram said.

"Well, I do," Zach said. "And so does anybody
who knows anything."

Zach got up from the table, grabbed his jacket,
and went out the door.

9

Bonfire Night

W here were you yesterday, Maggie? All the Irish kids were absent."

"At church."

"You don't have a church."

"The cellar's finished and the siding's up. We're getting things ready for the first Mass there."

"You can't have a church in a cellar."

"Better than the O'Reillys' front room."

"You've had Mass there?"

"We have."

"Are there windows?"

"Windows? In the O'Reillys' front room?"

"Eh-yah."

"Of course there are windows. Don't Yankees have windows in their front rooms?"

"Eh-yah. When are you having Mass in the cellar?"

"All Saints' Day."

"Is the Pope coming?"

"No, Charlotte. The Pope is in Rome. Somehow I don't think he'll make the journey to Westfield. We'll settle for a priest."

"Do you have pews and a pulpit in the cellar?"

"We'll have benches and an altar."

"Do you have a statue?"

"The Ahearns have a small one of the Blessed Virgin that they brought from the Old Country."

"And you worship the statue?"

"We don't worship it, Charlotte. We worship God. The statues help us remember the people who are near to God."

"But you have a secret ceremony?"

"It's not a secret. Anyone's welcome. You should come sometime."

"Not likely. Tonight is bonfire night, Maggie."

"Yes."

"Do you have food at your fire?"

"We do."

"So do we. Aunt Lucy and Bridget will be cooking all day, and I'll help as soon as I get home."

"And then Bridget will go help her family cook for our fire."

"Well, she likes cooking—I think."

"What will you make?"

"Pies, mostly. Just about every kind you can think of. Others are bringing deep dishes, and there'll be quadrille dancing. Mr. Dewey will call and fiddle."

"We'll probably have some dancing too."

"Quadrille?"

"More likely a jig or two. Hard to imagine you Yankees dancing and having fun."

"Of course we have fun Maggie. Why don't you come to our bonfire and see?"

"That'd be asking for trouble, Charlotte."

"No. No it won't."

"You don't think people will think hard of an Irish lass at a Yankee fire?"

"It isn't a Yankee fire, Maggie. It's an anybody fire."

"And all those people around it just happen to be Yankees?"

"Aunt Lucy and Uncle Hiram will be there. They won't let anything happen."

"I don't think so, Charlotte."

"There won't be any trouble because all the Irish except you will be up on the hill."

"All the Irish including me, I think."

"I tell you, even if people see you, they won't care."

"Let's see. All the Yankees in Westfield in one place talking about how they hate the Irish and look—here's an Irish girl over by the fountain."

"I don't think that will happen, Maggie."

"Indeed it won't, Charlotte."

❧

It rained hard all day, and Charlotte was afraid there'd be no bonfires at Park Square or on Prospect Hill, but the rain stopped in the late afternoon. At dusk the Hulls loaded up the carriage and drove the short distance down Broad Street. They could have walked, but they needed the carriage for all the pies and the fuel for the fire.

Most of the leaves had fallen from the trees, but

water still dripped from the remaining few. Park Square was bustling as people hurried from wagons and carriages: some men were setting up planks between sawhorses to serve as tables on a spot of green that seemed dry enough to hold them. Other men and boys brought wood and paper to add to the growing pile in the center of the square. Women carried food from all directions, stepping carefully around the puddles. Some were bringing chairs and dishes out of the church. People laughed and joked as they met each other going back and forth. Charlotte wished Maggie could see this. She'd see that Yankees knew how to have fun.

Aunt Lucy nudged her husband and pointed toward a group of men clustered around a barrel on the far side of the square. "Look, Hiram. They're drinking already. Tell them to take their drinking to the taverns."

"Oh, leave them to it, Lucy," Uncle Hiram said. "This is not the time or place for a temperance lecture."

"You children stay away from them, do you hear?" she told Zach and Charlotte. "I'm going to ask Reverend Cooper to speak to them.

Where is he? Do you see him anywhere?"

"No, Aunt Lucy," Charlotte said. Zach rolled his eyes, and Charlotte smiled. Despite her warning, Aunt Lucy seemed in as good a humor as everyone else tonight.

Uncle Hiram tied Regal's reins to the hitching post. Zach and Uncle Hiram began unloading the bonfire materials from the carriage. Aunt Lucy and Charlotte went back and forth from the carriage to the tables with the pies.

Mr. Zeb Carpenter seemed to be the self-appointed bonfire superintendent. "Put that box to the left of the oak stump, Bridgman!" he called out. "Not there! To the left! To the left!"

"Don't be so fussy, you old lady!" Mr. Bridgman called back, but he put the box where directed.

"Breaking up housekeeping, Jed?" Uncle Hiram asked as Mr. Brown added a chair to an assigned place on the pile.

"You bet," Mr. Brown replied. "Seat's so narrow on that thing that no one but Ethan can sit in it."

"Well, here's our three-legged table," Zach called. "It'll go up like tinder."

"Put it high on the right," Mr. Carpenter ordered.

Zach and Uncle Hiram swung the table back and forth between them and then heaved it. It tumbled back to the ground on the first try, but landed and stayed high on the pile the second time.

"Charlotte!" Mrs. Turner called out. "Come help us string apples." A long rope had been strung between two trees. Mrs. Turner, Ann, and Molly were tying apples by the stems to strings dangling from the rope. Later there'd be a contest to see who could take the most bites out of an apple without touching it with their hands.

"Yes," Ann said sweetly. "Come and help, Charlotte. We'll even give you the first turn."

"Um, I . . ." Charlotte stammered, trying wildly to think of an excuse.

"Oh, that does look like fun." Aunt Lucy was suddenly beside Charlotte. "But I need Charlotte's help over here," she said as she put her arm around Charlotte's shoulders and led her back to the carriage.

"Thank you, Aunt Lucy," Charlotte said. "I didn't want—"

"Of course you didn't. This is not the time," Aunt Lucy said, "but those girls will get their comeuppance. Just stand here for a minute and then head off in a different direction."

Uncle Hiram had sent men to bring boards and scraps of rattan and broken wooden boxes from the factory to add to the fire. The arrival of those wagons brought loud cheers from the crowd, and boys began unloading as soon as they pulled up.

Charlotte turned to examine the bonfire. It stood in the clearing, away from the elm trees that edged the square, and was now at least two stories high. Surely it was the biggest one ever, Charlotte thought. The fallen leaves, soaked with rain, had been raked up and were standing in baskets near the fire—to smother it if things got out of control, Mr. Carpenter said.

Charlotte wondered if Maggie would be able to see their flames from Prospect Hill. She looked around to get her bearings. Prospect Hill was a couple of miles to the northwest. She must remember to look in that direction when it got dark. Maybe she and Maggie could share both fires from a distance and talk about them tomorrow. Charlotte was relieved that everyone, even Zach, was in a good mood. There'd been so much fighting and tension these last few weeks that she had worried this celebration would be spoiled, but everything seemed just like it was last year, before the trouble began.

Clyde Dewey started up a tune on the fiddle and was quickly joined by another fiddler and a penny whistler. Little kids, mostly girls, linked arms and danced around in circles over by the fountain.

"Time for the quadrille! Form the squares!" Mr. Dewey called out when the first tune had ended. "I'll call the steps."

The crowd turned toward the makeshift stage where the musicians stood and then backed up to leave space for the dancing. This area was slightly higher than the rest of the green, and the puddles had been drained off. Hay had been scattered on the area to absorb the moisture, and now the damp hay had been raked aside.

"Come on now. Don't be shy," Mr. Dewey hollered when no one stepped forward to dance. "Who's the first head couple?"

To Charlotte's amazement and with the crowd's cheers, Hiram and Lucy Hull moved to the front, arm in arm.

"I guess that's us," Aunt Lucy said.

"Oh, good! They're touching each other," Charlotte exclaimed, and then clasped her hand over her mouth, but no one seemed to have heard her.

Uncle Hiram and Aunt Lucy turned, faced the crowd, and bowed. Three other couples joined them to make the first square, and then, with no further urging, three other squares were formed.

"Now that's more like it," Mr. Dewey said, and they struck up "Turkey in the Straw." "First couple leads to the folks across the way." And the dance began.

Charlotte clapped to the tune, exulting in the sight of her aunt and uncle as they turned and spun, their feet stepping out the beat. This was just wonderful! Who would have thought that they'd be such good dancers, and why hadn't they done it in other years?

The dance ended. Uncle Hiram leaned over and kissed his wife on the cheek. "Hiram," she protested. "Not in public." But she was laughing.

Charlotte ran up and hugged them. "Oh," she said. "Oh, that was lovely."

"Thank you, Peanut," Uncle Hiram said. "Lucy,

why don't you grab Zach, and I'll squire Charlotte for the next one."

Aunt Lucy headed toward Zach. In a minute she had dragged him over.

"I can't dance," Zach protested.

"Just listen to the caller," Aunt Lucy said. "You'll do fine."

Charlotte and Uncle Hiram laughed at Zach's discomfort, and the Walkers and the Carpenters completed their square.

"Address your partner," Mr. Dewey called out, and the music began again. "Allemande left with the lady on your left. Right hand to your partner and the grand right and left."

Even Zach began to smile as they moved around the square. The music was lively. Nobody seemed to care when somebody made a misstep. The non-dancers were clapping out the time.

"Now do-si-do that lady, and pass her to the right," Clyde called. "And when you meet your partner, go back where you've begun. Turn that lady round and promenade the hall."

Charlotte and Uncle Hiram spun, and the dance ended with everybody laughing.

"Thank you, Aunt Lucy," Zach said, bowing

politely, but he seemed relieved to head off toward a group of his friends by the apple bobbing.

"Thank you, kind lady," Uncle Hiram puffed as he bowed to Charlotte. "Got to sit the next one out. I'm winded." He headed toward the whiskey barrel.

"Hiram," Aunt Lucy said. "Don't—"

"Hiram! Hiram Hull! Where's Hiram?"

They turned to see Mr. Fowler waving from a wagon in front of the church. "Trouble at the factory, Hiram. Come a-running!"

Uncle Hiram ran toward the wagon and jumped in. Mr. Fowler flicked his whip, and the wagon headed up Elm Street.

"What can it be?" Charlotte asked. "What's happened?"

"I don't know," Aunt Lucy murmured, touching her fingertips to her lips as she stared after them. Then she turned as she shook her head. "Oh, don't fret, Charlotte." She seemed to be speaking to herself as much as to Charlotte. "It can't be too bad, or Sam would have asked for more than just your uncle."

Several men came over. "Do you know what's happened?" one asked.

"Does he need help, do you think?" asked another.

"I think if Hiram needs help, he knows where to find it," Aunt Lucy said. "Look. They're lighting the fire."

Aunt Lucy held Charlotte's hand as they stepped over to where men with torches were touching them to the pile under Mr. Carpenter's direction. Cheers and applause began, at first faintly and then with fervor as the flames took hold. Within minutes the entire pile seemed to glow from the inside out.

"That's some fire," Charlie Noble said. He was standing between Mr. Carpenter and Aunt Lucy. "Good job, Zeb."

Mr. Carpenter nodded. "You've got to lay it right, or the whole thing'll collapse and put itself out with everything so wet around here," he said with satisfaction. "It's all in how you set it up."

The musicians had come closer to the fire and struck up the lively Stephen Foster tune "Camptown Races." Zeb Carpenter began to sing, and people joined in first on the "doo-dahs" and then, gaining courage, started the second verse with him.

The next tune was less lively, "I Cannot Sing Tonight." People linked arms and swayed with the music. Several people began to sing the words, and soon others joined in. They were singing about not being able to sing. The thought made Charlotte smile, although the words were sad.

On the next verse Aunt Lucy picked up the alto part and a few men carried the bass. Charlotte wished she could harmonize, but she had a hard time even carrying the main tune. Harmony was far beyond her. How did they know which notes would sound good with the melody until they'd sung them? And by then it was too late. Maybe she'd learn that if she ever got to the Academy.

"My Old Kentucky Home" was the next song, and everyone sang.

> *Weep no more, my lady.*
> *Oh, weep no more today.*
> *For the sun shines bright*
> *On my Old Kentucky Home.*
> *My Old Kentucky Home far away.*

The crowd was silent after the last stroke of the violin, with everyone just gazing at the flames. Charlotte wished Uncle Hiram were here. It felt so good to feel all these happy people around her that she hardly gave a thought to those mean girls, who were somewhere in the crowd.

Then Mr. Tom Ashley stepped forward and faced them all. "This isn't Kentucky," he said. "But it's our Massachusetts home. And it's time to weep for what the Irish are doing to it." Some of the crowd cheered. Others turned and began to walk away.

"Don't turn away!" Tom Ashley shouted. "Thousands of Americans all over the country are joining the Know-Nothing Party. They're putting an end to the Irish Catholic takeover. Right here in Westfield, the Irish are in our streets. They've taken our jobs! They're in our schools! And now they're building a Catholic church right in the middle of Westfield. I say they've gone too far. And every decent God-fearing person here ought to be ready to stand up for what's right."

"Going to celebrate their heathen Mass in their cellar tomorrow," Mr. Clark yelled. "They worship statues. My son saw them at it."

"I did! I did!" Zenas Clark was jumping up and down. "Whit Warren saw it too! They were kneeling and praying to a statue!"

"Reverend Cooper! What does the leader of our faith say about that?" Mr. Ashley pointed toward the minister, who was standing a few rows back with his family. "What about the worshipers of statues? Isn't there something in the Good Book about that?"

"Thou shalt not make unto thee a graven image, nor any manner of likeness, of any thing that is in heaven above," Reverend Cooper's voice rang out.

"It's an abomination! It is the work of the devil himself."

"Oh, good heavens," Aunt Lucy murmured. "Now he speaks up. That's all we need."

"Hear that? The work of the devil, the reverend says. What are we going to do about it?" Mr. Ashley shouted.

Aunt Lucy said, "It's time to go home, Charlotte. Where's Zach?"

"I don't know," Charlotte said, looking around. "He was over there with some boys, but I can't see any of them now."

"Those Micks have taken every job in town," Mr. Ashley continued.

"They're taking over the whole country," a female voice shouted.

"They're trying to convert our children to their statue worshiping," said another.

Mr. John Marshall stepped up beside Mr. Ashley. He had an unlit torch in his hand. "The Irish took my job! Good, decent Protestants are taking orders now from the Micks! Rise up! Now's the time!" he shouted. "Light up your torches, men. I know where there's something better to burn." He turned to light his torch from the bonfire.

"They're all up on the hill. We can burn every house on Meadow Street!"

"We'll burn the church!"

"First the church and then the houses. Burn them all out! Get rid of every last Mick in town. Send them back to Ireland, where they belong!"

The shouting grew as more men lit torches. "Every decent God-fearing man step forward!" someone shouted. "Ladies and children too. Let's show the damned Irish what hellfire looks like."

Aunt Lucy had her arm around Charlotte. "Come quickly," she said. "Hurry."

"What about Zach?" Charlotte asked.

Aunt Lucy said, "No time. Come on, Charlotte."

They ran to the carriage. In seconds Aunt Lucy had

turned Regal, and the carriage rumbled over the cobblestones on Elm Street.

"But home is the other way," Charlotte said, holding on tight. She didn't know Regal could gallop so fast.

"Home can wait," Aunt Lucy said. "We've got to get Hiram. He's got to stop those fools."

They turned left when they got to the river and pulled through the factory gates. Mr. Fowler's horse whinnied, and Regal answered as Aunt Lucy threw the reins over the hitching post. She and Charlotte ran toward the factory.

"Over there," Charlotte shouted as she spotted lantern light in one of the basement windows.

Aunt Lucy knelt and pounded on the window. "Hiram!" she shouted. "Hiram!"

The lantern light came closer, and Uncle Hiram's and Mr. Fowler's faces peered up at them.

"What?"

"Come!"

The lantern light grew faint as Uncle Hiram and Mr. Fowler headed for the stairs. In a minute they were at the door.

"Who's hurt?" Uncle Hiram asked.

"Nobody's hurt," Charlotte said. He was

soaking wet, and so was Mr. Fowler.

Aunt Lucy said, "They're going to burn the church!"

"And their houses!" Charlotte added.

"What? The Irish church?" Mr. Fowler asked.

"Yes! Come on, you two! They've got everybody all stirred up. You've got to stop them."

"I can't," Uncle Hiram said. "There's a leak in the river wall. Water's pouring in."

"Then let Sam come," his wife said. "It's bad, Hiram, and getting worse."

"Can't spare him," Uncle Hiram said. "I was going to go for more help here." He looked back toward the square, where the bonfire flames lit up the sky. "You've got to get the Irish, Lucy."

"Me? No, Hiram, I . . ." Aunt Lucy stammered.

"They're probably all drunk."

"Find Mike Nolan," Uncle Hiram said. "Tell him to get everybody to the church. Sam and I will get there as soon as we plug the leak."

For a moment Aunt Lucy just stared at her husband. Charlotte grabbed her aunt's hand and pulled her toward the carriage. "Come on, Aunt Lucy. They're up on the hill," she said.

"I can't do this," Charlotte heard Aunt Lucy whisper as they galloped along.

"Somebody's got to," Charlotte said.

"What have we done?" her aunt said softly. "What have we done?"

"I don't think we did anything," Charlotte said through chattering teeth.

"We talked," Aunt Lucy said. "Or at least I did."

"Well, talking doesn't hurt anyone," Charlotte chattered. "Does it?"

In minutes they were crossing the Westfield River Bridge. There the cobblestones gave way to dirt. They turned sharp left to go up the hill. The few houses near the road were all in darkness.

"Where's their fire?" Aunt Lucy asked.

Charlotte looked around frantically. "Maggie just said it was on the hill."

Aunt Lucy cupped her hands and hollered, "Help! Help!"

There was no answering sound or movement. In the pale moonlight all they could see were woods, fields, and darkened houses.

Charlotte pointed toward the woods. "It's lighter over there," she said.

"Where's the road in?" Aunt Lucy said. "I can't get the carriage through those trees." She took a lantern from under the seat, lit it, and handed it to Charlotte. "Take this," she said, "and see if you can find a path or a road through those trees."

Now they could hear shouting as the light through the trees grew brighter. *They must have lit the fire*, Charlotte thought as she ran toward the trees. The undergrowth was thick, and she could see no way through it. Then the lantern light shone on a patch of dirt. Two steps more and she saw a path.

"Here!" Charlotte shouted. "Over here, Aunt Lucy."

Aunt Lucy hurried over. "Quick, Charlotte," she said. "Run ahead. See if you can find your friend. She'll know where her father is."

Charlotte hesitated. "Can't we both go?"

"Run ahead," Aunt Lucy repeated. "Your young legs will go faster than mine. I'm right behind you."

Charlotte nodded and began to run, the lantern bouncing up and down in her hand. Behind her she could hear Aunt Lucy's hurried steps, then a crash. Charlotte turned to see her aunt sprawled on the ground.

"Aunt Lucy!" She hurried back to her.

Aunt Lucy waved away Charlotte's hand. "I'm all right," she said as she struggled to her feet. "Run on. Keep going!"

Now Charlotte could see the backs of people facing a bonfire. She could hear laughing and talking. Music was playing, and she could see people dancing. How would she ever find Maggie Nolan? Maybe she should just tell whomever she saw first. She ran up to a woman standing with a group of children.

"Where's Maggie Nolan?" she asked.

"Maggie? Heavens! Who knows?" the woman answered.

"Her father then," Charlotte said. "Do you know where Mike Nolan is?"

"And who might you be?"

"Please," Charlotte said. "I really need to find them."

"Maggie was over there," one of the children said, motioning toward another group. Charlotte ran over.

"Maggie!" she shouted. "Maggie Nolan!"

Behind her she could barely hear her aunt calling, "Mike Nolan! Is Mike Nolan here?"

Suddenly two boys stood in front of Charlotte. "Well, here she is again, looking for trouble," one of them said.

Charlotte gasped. They were the same boys who had taken the barley.

"Yeah," said the other. "Welcome back, little Yankee girl in the wrong place again. And no Jack O'Malley to get in the way this time. What shall we do with her?" He grabbed Charlotte's arm.

Charlotte tried to pull away, but the boy's grip was strong. "Oh, please, don't! I need to find Maggie Nolan," she pleaded.

"Maggie's busy," the other boy said as he grabbed Charlotte's other arm. "Let's us go over behind this barn where we can talk." They half led, half carried Charlotte away from the crowd, which was too intent on the fire to know or care what was going on behind it. Charlotte struggled as her feet dragged along the ground.

"Won't that be fun?" The other boy turned to grin at Charlotte.

"Please, please, let me go," Charlotte begged. "There's trouble—"

"No trouble. It will be fun. Say 'Eh-yah,'" the first boy demanded. He shook her arm roughly.

"Come on. Say 'Eh-yah.'"

Suddenly the second boy yelled, "Owww!" and let go of Charlotte's arm as he fell to the ground. The other boy was shoved forward as Aunt Lucy yanked his arm away from Charlotte.

Aunt Lucy had her foot on the second boy's back. "Where's Mike Nolan?" she demanded.

"Hey!" the boy yelled. "Let me up! How do I know where he is?"

The other boy ran off as Aunt Lucy hoisted her capture to his feet. She held his arm and his right ear.

"Ow!" he yelled. "Let me go!"

Aunt Lucy was propelling him back toward the crowd, Charlotte at her side. "Now," said Aunt Lucy when they got near enough. "You and I and Charlotte are all going to yell 'Mike Nolan' when I count to three."

"I will n—" the boy began. "Owwww!"

"One, two, three," Aunt Lucy counted, and the three of them yelled in one voice, "Mike Nolan," although the boy's yell was more of an "Owwwwww."

"What?" a voice from the crowd yelled back. Aunt Lucy let go of the boy's arm as a man came toward them out of the crowd. The boy scooted away.

"I'm Mike," he said. "And who are you?"

"Charlotte!" came a familiar voice, and Maggie ran up. "What are you doing here?"

"Trouble," Aunt Lucy said before Charlotte could do anything but grasp her friend's arm. "You've got to get to the church, Mike. They're going to burn it."

"Burn what? Our church? Who is?"

"Everybody," Charlotte broke in. "Everybody down there is mad or drunk or something. They're going to burn it, Maggie."

Mike nodded and, without another word, ran to a small platform over by the bonfire. "Hey!" he yelled. "Everyone to the church. The Yankees are on the march. Grab whatever you can and run."

Suddenly everybody was shouting and dashing about. Maggie gave one quick squeeze on Charlotte's hand and ran off.

"What shall we do now?" Charlotte asked.

"This way," Aunt Lucy said, and they hurried back down the path, but Regal and their carriage were not where they'd left them.

"Regall!" Charlotte exclaimed, peering around in the darkness.

"They've taken him," Aunt Lucy said. "Can't say that I blame them. Come on, Charlotte. It's shank's mare for us."

They started back to the top of the hill, but were scarcely there when Aunt Lucy stopped. "Wait, Charlotte," she gasped. "Got to catch my breath."

"I'll go ahead," Charlotte said.

"No," Aunt Lucy said between breaths. "No, Charlotte. Too many people are too riled up for you to be by yourself. We'll get there. It's only about a mile. We'll stay together."

The way down to Bartlett Street seemed endless. It was hard for Charlotte not to tug on Aunt Lucy's arm to hurry her along. People ran past them, some shoving against them as they went by.

At last they got to the corner of Bartlett and Elm. Looking down the short street, they could see shadows of the mob clustered around the partly built church cellar, the torches waving back and forth.

"Hurry, Aunt Lucy," Charlotte said. "Don't stop now. We're nearly there."

"And here we stop," Aunt Lucy declared. "There's no telling what will happen. We've done our job. There's a lot of Irish down there now. We're heading for home as soon as I get my breath."

"Regal!" Charlotte exclaimed. "We've got to find Regal, Aunt Lucy. He must be scared."

"Takes more than a crowd to scare that horse," Aunt Lucy said. "He'll be fine."

"He's been run hard," Charlotte protested. "He'll need rubbing down and blanketing." Charlotte took her aunt's hand. "Come on, Aunt Lucy. Let's find Regal."

"Regal will find his own way home. He's probably there waiting for us now." Aunt Lucy refused to move.

"But we've got to help," Charlotte said. "We've got to stop them from burning the church."

"Let the Irish defend their own," Aunt Lucy said.

"But there's more Yankees than Irish," Charlotte said. "We outnumber them."

"Well, not every Yankee is down there making trouble. Thank goodness some of them had better sense. It's in God's hands," Aunt Lucy said. "We'll go no closer, Charlotte."

"What about Zach?" Charlotte asked. She felt guilty for not thinking of Zach before this. "He may be in the middle of this." She started down the street, pulling Aunt Lucy.

"Oh, Lord! I'd forgotten Zach."

"There he is!" Charlotte said, tugging her forward. They were nearly at the church. "I see him! He's got a torch."

"Where? I don't see him. Oh, that boy!"

"Over there by that group of boys! He's right at the corner of the cellar. See him?" Charlotte and Aunt Lucy were now at the back of the mob of Yankees. Although most of them were men and boys, there were a few women and girls as well. Boards had been placed over the cellar, making a kind of roof.

"Zach!" Aunt Lucy yelled, but her voice was lost in the chorus of shouts.

Peering around the people in front of her, Charlotte could see that Irish men, women, and children had linked arms in a ring around the entire church facing the mob. Charlotte could see Maggie standing beside a woman holding two babies in her arms. Maggie was crying, and so were lots of others as they faced the crowd. Others were shouting, although there was so much racket Charlotte couldn't make out what was said. Some boys were trying to drag the Irish away from the foundation, but, as one fell or was pulled from the ring, another arrived to take the place.

Tom Ashley pushed his way to the front of the mob. He turned to face them. "Time to light the best bonfire of the night!"

"Yay! Light it up!"

"You'll have to kill us first!" a man standing at the church shouted back.

"That's not a problem," John Marshall said with a grin. "Happy to oblige!"

Charlotte could see the determination and glee on Zach's face as he leaned forward to touch his fire to the roof boards. Whit had pushed people aside there so that a small space opened up between the defenders. A hand on Zach's arm stopped him. Uncle Hiram! He took the torch from Zach, turned to douse it in a puddle, and then stepped up beside Tom Ashley.

"Even Hiram Hull is with us tonight," Mr. Ashley declared. "He's had enough just like the rest of us. Let's hear from Hiram!" He smiled, and holding his torch high in his right hand, put his left arm around Uncle Hiram's shoulders. Hiram Hull twisted his body as he stepped forward. Mr. Ashley's arm fell, and his smile wilted.

"I do have something to say." Uncle Hiram sounded out of breath. "And I'm glad to have a chance to say it." He made a move to step up on the roof. Two men pushed him back, but Maggie's father motioned them aside and gave Uncle Hiram an arm to help him up. Hiram Hull faced the crowd; he wasn't shouting, but as the crowd quieted, his voice rang out.

"What are we doing here?" he asked as he held his arms out as if to embrace the crowd before him. "Some of the people here tonight are just boys who probably heard some of us saying things we shouldn't have said. Some of us, I'm afraid, don't have youth as an excuse, but we get riled up. We lose our heads." He looked down and then up at the crowd again. "At any rate, we've got folks all stirred up, and even my nephew Zachary's here with a torch. I'm ashamed to say that he thought he should burn down a house of worship. He should know better." Uncle Hiram paused and looked down again for a moment. "Actually, the shame is mine," he said as he looked up again. "I ought to have taught him better."

"Get him down from there!" someone shouted.

"Light the damned thing up and be done with it!"

Charlotte looked around in the torchlight at the shouters. These were her neighbors—people who had sat at their table with kind faces and soft voices—well, some of them had, anyway. Now those same faces were twisted and ugly.

Uncle Hiram went on as if no one had spoken. He was looking not in Zach's direction but at the crowd of Yankees. "You see, these young ones don't know enough. We haven't told them enough about how it was before. And that's the school's fault, your fault, and my fault." Uncle Hiram nodded as if agreeing with himself. "I can't tell Zach or anyone else about the Irish because I'm ashamed to say I just don't know enough about them. But I think their tale isn't all that different from mine. I should have told Zach a Yankee tale. I should have told him how my people—his people—came here because they couldn't make a go of it in England." Uncle Hiram shook his head. "They couldn't get work. They couldn't own land. They crowded into what few houses they could afford—sometimes three or four families to a house. They didn't believe what the people around them said about God and about the way they should worship. They held church in each other's houses because they weren't allowed to build their own church. And the people with power thought my people had no rights. So after a while my folks left England. They came first to Boston and then to this spot by the river to start afresh. They cleared the land, fought the Indians, built the town, built their church."

No one spoke, but there was a kind of shuffling as people shifted about. Then came a hissing sound as two men with torches walked over to douse them in a puddle.

"And you and I made it better." Uncle Hiram's voice was proud. "We built the shops, ran the businesses, built the schools. I should have told Zach that." He nodded as if speaking to himself. "I should have told Zach that," he repeated. "Zach would surely have acted differently tonight if he had known those things."

The crowd was completely quiet. "Go to it, Hiram," Aunt Lucy whispered. She was biting her lower lip, and tears were running down her cheeks. The darkness grew as more men doused their torches.

Charlotte looked around again at the crowd. Some were looking at Uncle Hiram, but most of them were looking at the ground.

"So, I'm glad we've gathered here tonight," Uncle Hiram said in a more cheerful voice. "Now Zach knows some of what he needs to know. I'll teach him more if he'll let me. This torchlight parade is a good way to get things going in the right direction, to wish our Irish friends good luck. I wish we could all stay and celebrate, but we need every able-bodied man and boy to hurry with me to the river, for it has decided to explore our fine town on its own. If we don't start stacking sandbags against it soon, we'll have Lake Westfield and no town with any churches."

With that, Uncle Hiram jumped down, put his arm around Zach, and, although Zach tried to pull away, hurried him down the street. Most of the men and boys followed Hiram Hull to the river, and the others walked slowly away.

10

After

I couldn't believe it was you standing there."

"Oh, Maggie. It was so scary. Those boys—"

"They're just mean thugs. Your aunt Lucy's something, isn't she?"

"She's wonderful. So's your father."

"And what about your uncle?"

"Eh-yah. That was amazing. Was your whole family in that circle?"

"Yes. Even the twins."

"Weren't you scared?"

"Couldn't you see my knees shaking?"

"Maggie, I'm so sorry."

"Why? What did you do?"

"Not me. Those Yankees. I'm so sorry."

"You did everything you could to stop it, Charlotte."

"But it was so awful. I couldn't believe they'd try to burn down your church, Maggie."

"They didn't all try. Da says about fifty. So a good many Yankees had no part in it."

"But so many did."

"Aye. It was a Yankee who gave the land, Yankees who tried to burn it, and a Yankee who stopped them."

"That and a ring of Irish and the flood."

"Who'd have thought a flood could be a good thing?"

"Did your house get flooded, Maggie?"

"Only the cellar. We were lucky. The O'Reillys had to stay with us. They have water up to the second floor."

"The O'Reillys? How many people?"

"Six. My brothers had to carry their granny over. She can't walk."

"How did you find room enough?"

"Mam said Noah found room for more. We made do. How's Zach?"

"I don't know, Maggie. He stayed at Whit's last night."

"What will you say to him when you see him?"

"I don't know, Maggie. I don't know."

❧

After school Charlotte headed for the Warrens' house on Franklin Street. It would make her very late getting home, but she had to talk with Zach.

"I don't know where he is," Whit said in answer to her question. "When I got up, he was gone."

"Didn't he tell you where he was going?"

"He didn't tell me anything, Charlotte. He wouldn't talk at all. Just crawled into bed when we got home from the factory. We were all exhausted from packing sandbags most of the night."

"Maybe he went home," Charlotte offered hopefully.

"Maybe," Whit said. He turned and went back inside.

But there was no sign of Zach at home—no sign of anybody. They must be out looking for Zach. Charlotte would be searching too if she only knew where to look. She sat down to talk to Thomas and Rachel, but their faces offered no comfort.

She jumped up when she heard Regal's hooves on the road. "Did you find him?" she asked, even though, to her disappointment, Aunt Lucy was alone in the carriage.

"No, dear," her aunt replied as she looped Regal's reins on the post. "I've looked everywhere I can think of. Nobody's seen him."

"He will come home, won't he?"

"Of course he will. He'll come home. He's got no place else to go."

Supper was late because Uncle Hiram was late. He shook his head to Aunt Lucy's silent inquiry of raised eyebrows when at last he came in the door.

Aunt Lucy set a place for Zach at the table, and it seemed that both she and Charlotte stared at that place through supper. At last Charlotte could stand it no longer.

"Where can he be?"

Uncle Hiram, the only one who appeared to have an appetite, mopped the last of the gravy on his plate with his bread, wiped his lips with his napkin, and said, "I don't know, Charlotte. If he wanted us to find him, we would have."

"But he will come home, won't he? He has to, doesn't he?" Charlotte was determined not to cry, but her eyes brimmed with tears.

"Of course he will, child." Aunt Lucy reached over to grasp Charlotte's hand. "He'll be home very soon, I know."

"I wish I were that sure," Uncle Hiram said.

"He's got a lot of thinking to do. He's angry, and he's embarrassed, or should be, by what happened. He needs to come to grips with that in his own way. We can't help him do that, Charlotte."

"How long will that take?" Charlotte asked.

"Only Zach knows that," her uncle said.

"But eventually?"

"Of course he'll come home," Aunt Lucy repeated, but Charlotte thought her words lacked conviction.

"Well," Uncle Hiram said, "he wouldn't be the first boy to strike out on his own. He's strong and healthy. He can find work and make a life for himself if he chooses."

"No!" Aunt Lucy exclaimed. "He's just a child."

"You and your brother were working in a factory by the time you were Zach's age, Lucy, and many of my workers are no older."

"That was for lack of money," Aunt Lucy said.

"There's no need here."

"And Zach knows where there's a warm bed and good food whenever he chooses to take it," Uncle Hiram said.

"But you'll keep looking, won't you?" Charlotte asked. "We'll all keep looking, won't we?"

"We'll keep our eyes open and the door unlocked," Uncle Hiram said. "In the meantime, life goes on. Isn't there a school board meeting tonight, Lucy?"

"Yes, Hiram," she said. "And I mean to go. There's the Miss Avery matter to bring up."

"Indeed," Uncle Hiram said. "Let's go."

"You're going?" Charlotte and Aunt Lucy asked in unison.

"Wouldn't miss it for the world," he said.